REUNITED WITH
HER ITALIAN
BILLIONAIRE

REUNITED WITH HER ITALIAN BILLIONAIRE

NINA SINGH

MILLS & BOON

First published in Great Britain 2018
by Mills & Boon, an imprint of HarperCollins*Publishers*
1 London Bridge Street, London, SE1 9GF

Large Print edition 2018

© 2018 Nilay Nina Singh

ISBN: 978-0-263-07384-3

MIX
Paper from
responsible sources
FSC™ C007454

This book is produced from independently certified FSC™ paper to ensure responsible forest management. For more information visit www.harpercollins.co.uk/green.

Printed and bound in Great Britain
by CPI Group (UK) Ltd, Croydon, CR0 4YY

To my parents—you always said I could.

CHAPTER ONE

SHE SHOULD HAVE known he would come.

The dark, commanding man at her back door was the last person Brianna wanted to see. Though she should have guessed. Marco Dirici had a knack for showing up in her life unbidden and unwelcome.

Brianna peeked through the side window again. She knew it was him. The voice had confirmed it. Still, she couldn't help but wish that maybe if she looked again it would be someone else standing there.

No such luck. It was definitely Marco, in the flesh. Not that she was surprised. He wasn't the kind of man to stay away.

Brianna looked down at the worn gray T-shirt she was wearing and swiped at the dark smudges under her eyes. Great. Six long months since she'd last seen him and he had to catch her on a morning when she looked her absolute worst.

But what did it matter anyhow? She no longer cared what she looked like in front of Marco. Except that he was immaculate as usual. The leather jacket he wore brought out the black of his eyes. His dark hair fell over his forehead the way she remembered. It hadn't been that long ago that she'd taken great pleasure in gently stroking that wayward lock off his face, only to have it fall forward again.

"Brianna, open the door. I know you're in there." His voice sounded from the other side of the door, dripping with that sexy Italian accent that haunted her dreams.

"*Cara*, open the door," Marco repeated. "I don't want to have to ring the bell. Little Enzo is probably still sleeping."

At the mention of her son, Brianna forgot all about her appearance and her apprehension. Two-year-old Lorenzo was the reason Marco was here.

Slowly, she unlatched the lock and stepped aside to let her husband in.

Marco brushed past her without so much as a glance.

"What took you so long? I had to go around the back when you didn't answer the front door."

She'd been in a deep sleep. Enzo had kept her up half the night refusing to go into his crib.

He gave her a stern look when she didn't answer. "I thought the little old lady across the street was going to come at me with a broom. I'm positive she thinks I'm here to commit some kind of crime."

Are you?

Brianna shoved the door closed and turned to face him. "What in the world are you doing here?"

"What do you think? I spoke to Nonna."

Of course. She should have never made that phone call to Marco's grandmother. But Brianna had been truly desperate for some advice from someone else who loved and cared about Enzo.

"You shouldn't be here," she answered.

"I grew tired of waiting for you to come to your senses," he said. "And I missed my son. What did you expect me to do?"

A small part of her wanted to hear that he'd missed her as well. But that was such a silly thought. He wanted nothing to do with her. He never really had. As she stood aching inside at seeing him again.

If it was possible, he was even more handsome than she remembered. Those dark eyes she'd lost herself in so many times in the past were as deep as always. She couldn't lose herself again. Not to this man. Not ever. She had given him too much of herself already.

"I didn't expect you to do anything." She walked over to the baby monitor on the counter and turned it up, just to give herself something to do. "Only to respect my wishes and give Enzo and me the time we need."

"You've been gone for six months."

"Nothing has changed, Marco. You've wasted a trip across the world for no reason."

"You want a divorce, *cara*. I am not divorcing my child."

Brianna stiffened. "That's not fair. You know that's the last thing I want."

He let out a laugh which sounded far from amused. "Is that what you call hauling him thousands of miles away?"

She took a deep breath. "Look, when I left I promised you we'd come to a fair agreement about visitation. Until we do that, you can't just show up here unannounced. You can see him at designated times or not at all."

He was in front of her in an instant, hardly an inch of space separating them. "I don't think so. You throw me crumbs and then have the nerve to threaten those measly bits. That I cannot allow you to do."

Brianna's heart pounded. She had to stand up to him. "Don't fight me on this, Marco. I need to make a clean break."

He took her hand in a gentle but firm grip. "I won't let go of my son, Brianna."

Any hope she had that Marco might have changed over the past few months evaporated. "And I don't want that either. I'm sorry you don't understand."

He sighed and dropped her hand. "You're right. I don't understand it. I don't understand why your desire to cook for others in New York City overrides your desire to be my wife back in Italy. I certainly don't understand why you needed to leave."

He was certainly right about that. He never did understand. "I had no choice."

"So you seem to believe."

For the briefest moment, Brianna thought she saw utter weariness in his face. But the look was gone in an instant. Perhaps she had imagined it.

"No, you're wrong. I couldn't have been a good mother to Enzo being as unhappy as I was."

"And this." He gestured around the small house. "This is what makes you happy?"

Brianna crossed her arms in front of her chest. She didn't know how to answer that. No, she wasn't happy. Things hadn't worked out at all the way they were supposed to since she'd moved back to New York. Mostly, and to her utter horror, her son had so far not adjusted well at all.

But those last months in Italy, things had just been getting colder and colder between them. In fact, they weren't even pretending to be an actual married couple anymore. Simply two people living under the same roof. That was what happened when one tried to force a family into existence. She should have known better.

Still, she hadn't expected to miss Marco as much as she did.

He looked at her expectantly. His next words made her wonder if he'd somehow read her mind about missing him. "So tell me what makes you happy, *cara*." His dark, smoldering eyes fell to her lips.

He stepped closer. Brianna forced herself to look away. If she wasn't careful, she could so easily fall into the Marco Dirici trap again. His voice, that look.

"Do you remember being happy at least at first?" he asked.

And what kind of a question was that?

As if she could forget. Her mind automatically recalled the first time he'd kissed her. They'd met only hours before. Yet, she couldn't resist his charm and sheer magnetism. She hardly recognized herself that night and the following week after meeting him.

A small wailing sound from the monitor jarred her back and she glanced at the wall. "Now see what you've done? He's awake. It's at least an hour until his usual wake-up time."

Marco sighed then stepped away from her. Was that a hint of disappointment she detected in his eyes? Probably not.

"I'd like to see my son."

Brianna took a steadying breath and waited a

beat for the pounding in her chest to slow. Then she made her way toward the stairs.

Marco watched her walk away and cursed himself. After six months without laying eyes on her, the second he'd seen her again he'd felt like a damn hormonal teenager. The same way he had close to three years ago. And just like back then, it had only taken one look at her. Her emerald-green eyes still blazed, just as he remembered. And her lips. Heavens, those lips reminded him of sin. Her nightwear left little to the imagination. But he already knew every inch of her. She was exquisite, she was stunning. And for a while, she had been his.

But never completely.

What was it about this woman that made him lose such control? The last thing he'd had on his mind when he'd walked in here was to travel down memory lane and reminisce about the first time he'd laid eyes on her.

He rubbed his brow. He couldn't let his attraction to her complicate matters on this trip. The attraction was merely physical. Same as always.

He needed more from her than she was willing to give. He'd never begged a woman for anything.

He certainly wasn't going to start with his soon-to-be ex-wife. And certainly not to delay the inevitable.

He had only two reasons to be here: to tell Brianna she could have the divorce she so wanted and, most importantly, to work out final custody of Enzo. His son was all that mattered now. He'd never really expected Brianna to stay around. Women came and women went. But *familia*... He would fight to keep his blood.

He looked around the house he knew she rented. The kitchen was tidy, with a small round table in the center. Through an arched doorway he could see a living room with a center sitting area. A bay window overlooked the street. The house was small, modest.

There was nothing overtly wrong with the place, but it certainly didn't compare to the expansive mansion Brianna had lived in as his wife.

She preferred it here.

Not that he was surprised. His arrival in her life three years ago had served to totally derail it. At that time she had just landed a new job, was working hard to make a name for herself in the New York culinary world. Then he'd come along and disrupted it all. Before they knew it and to their combined utter shock, they found themselves unwed and expecting. He'd asked her to marry him and join him in Italy. For a while it seemed as if the union might work. But it quickly became obvious they were headed down a rocky road.

For one, Brianna had a difficult pregnancy. Passion, the one thing that bound them, had to be put on hold. And the expansion of Dirici Foods had hit snag after snag, taking him away from home consistently.

Still, Marco had hoped she would fall in love with her new home. That she would try to acclimate and settle into the new life she found herself in, regardless of how unexpectedly it had come about. But that had not happened. He never should have expected it. Foolish, really.

Something tightened in his gut. The time had simply come to cut his losses.

He had to finalize things with her in New York quickly, and then he had to get out of her life as best he could.

* * *

The hard children's book hurtling toward Brianna missed her head by mere inches. She rose from her ducked position as the book bounced against the wall with a thud and landed on the floor.

"Now! Now! Now!"

"Enzo, we don't throw things at Mama," Brianna scolded. A teddy bear hit her on the chest.

"Do you want me to start taking your favorite toys out of your crib?"

"Out! Now!"

Brianna picked up the screaming child and held him close, hoping to calm him down. Enzo smelled of baby shampoo and the delicate scent of talc.

Even during moments like this, Brianna couldn't believe the sheer wave of emotion that holding her child brought forth. She'd never expected to have a child at this stage of her life. But she was grateful beyond words to have him. Especially considering the terrifying touch-and-go moments that plagued her pregnancy. She'd prayed daily that her precious little boy would be born full term and healthy, so thankful finally when he had.

"Keech!" Enzo shouted in her ear.

"We'll go down to the kitchen in a moment," Brianna said. "But first I need to tell you something." She set him down.

Enzo ran toward the stairs, not listening at all. She followed close behind. He hadn't quite mastered going down the steps yet but that never slowed him down.

"Enzo, wait."

He was already pulling open the unlocked safety gate at the top of the stairs when Brianna caught up to him.

"Keech! Keech!"

"All right, all right." Brianna took his hand and slowly, carefully walked him down the stairs. "We're going down there now. There's someone here to see you."

As soon as they reached the first-floor landing, he ran to the kitchen.

"Joos!"

When he spotted Marco, Enzo came to a sudden halt. Brianna noticed the thinly veiled derision in Marco's expression as he lifted Enzo into his arms.

The baby monitor. Marco had overheard her and Enzo's little exchange.

"Hi!" Enzo said loudly, grabbing Marco's collar. "Joos!"

"Hey, little man," Marco said, rubbing his cheek against Enzo's. "Did you miss Papa?"

Her chest tightened at the scene and at Marco's words. She had no reason to feel guilty. She couldn't have stayed any longer in a marriage that wasn't working, one that had simply originated out of necessity because of pregnancy. Sure, it had been painful to take Enzo away from Italy and his papa. Not to mention the doting great-grandmother who adored him. But Brianna was slowly becoming a mere shell of herself there. That was no way to raise a child. Especially considering she was doing most of it on her own with Marco gone long hours for days on end.

"He likes to sit by the window and drink it while I get his breakfast ready," she said, handing Enzo a full sippy cup.

Marco sighed and put his son down. Enzo immediately scuttled to the love seat in front of the bay window.

"Do you suppose he remembers me?" Marco asked.

"I'm sure he does."

Marco looked skeptical. His eyes bored into hers. "I'm glad one of us is sure."

The implication was clear. There was no doubt in her mind who Marco would blame if Enzo in fact didn't remember him.

CHAPTER TWO

BRIANNA CHOSE TO try and ignore the tension in the air. Pushing her way around Marco to grab the bread off the counter, she dropped two slices into the toaster and stared at it, as if toasting bread took the utmost concentration. All the while she could feel Marco's gaze on her back.

"I have to get to the restaurant today," she said. "You'll have to find a way to keep yourself busy."

She moved to the refrigerator for the butter. Marco stood directly in front of it. He, of course, refused to budge. She brushed past him, the slight physical contact just enough to inflame her nerves.

"I'll stay right here with my son," Marco said.

Opening the door as wide as she could with him standing there, Brianna reached for the butter drawer. "I'm afraid not."

"I beg your pardon?"

"Enzo's nanny will be here any minute. She usually has the whole day planned for him."

He shrugged. "You can give her the day off."

Brianna slowly shut the refrigerator door. "It's too late to do that. She's probably on the train right now."

"So tell her when she gets here. I don't see a problem."

"I'm not going to tell her she's wasted a trip. Or that she'll have to miss a day of compensation."

Marco looked up to the ceiling and sighed. His expression made him look every bit the part of a man holding on to the last of his patience. "I'll compensate her for the commute and give her two days' pay for her trouble. A week's pay."

That was so typical of Marco. "You think you can solve anything with money."

"I've found very few issues money couldn't solve," he replied, his voice hard.

"Well, this is my home and I won't allow it," she declared just as the doorbell rang.

At the sound, Enzo jumped up and yelled "Ding-dong!"

Brianna barely caught him before he tumbled

off the cushion onto the floor. He wailed in protest. The doorbell rang again. And again.

"I'm coming. I'm coming." Brianna set Enzo
down gently on his feet. Marco gave her another
amused smirk.

She scowled back and opened the door. "Mrs.
Schelling. You're here."

Her nanny trotted inside and let out a loud
"hmmph" before turning to her. "I only came
for one thing, and then I'll be going." The grim
set of the woman's lips sent alarms ringing in
Brianna's head.

Not now, not today. She forced a smile, almost
certain she knew what was about to happen. "Oh.
All right. Why don't we go talk in the kitchen?"

"There's nothing to talk about. I've come to
quit."

Brianna's heart dived. Somehow she kept her
smile in place. Putting her arm around the other
woman's plump shoulders, she tried to move her
toward the kitchen. Away from Marco.

"Don't even joke like that, Mrs. Schelling."

Mrs. Schelling didn't move. "This is no joke,
Miss Brianna. I refuse to tolerate any more from
that young man." Squinting, she pointed to Enzo.

Enzo in turn stopped sucking on his cup long enough to give Mrs. Schelling a wide grin.

"I don't understand." Brianna dropped her arm.

Mrs. Schelling held out her palm. "I quit and I'd like my remaining payment."

"But why?"

"I can no longer take care of your son. Life is too short. And I'm afraid I've already lived the bulk of mine at my age."

Brianna didn't dare look at Marco. She had no doubt what he had to be thinking. In his eyes, she had failed him as his wife and now she was clearly failing as a single mother.

This was the last impression she would have hoped to give upon seeing him again. Rather than proving her independence and abilities, she was instead coming off as flighty and in disarray, unable to get her act straight.

All she'd ever wanted was a stable home, some roots. With the arrival of her son, that had seemed like a real possibility. But now it was all going to rot somehow. She may have ended up with a family but it had come about in a random and haphazard manner. Now even that was falling apart.

"I've been thinking about this all night. Agonizing over the decision," Mrs. Schelling was saying. Listening to her was like trying to focus as the walls crumbled around her. Brianna had tried so hard to lay the groundwork perfectly for her return to the United States. All to watch it implode now. And just her luck, Marco was here to witness the latest catastrophe.

The older woman paused to take a deep breath. "Your son is simply too much for me to handle. I dare say he's too much for anyone to handle."

Now that was a bit much. Brianna looked directly into the older woman's eyes. "He's barely two. He just doesn't know any better."

Mrs. Schelling took a tiny step back. Maybe it was the edge that had crept into her voice. It was a small source of satisfaction.

"Nevertheless, I don't have to put up with his behavior. Not for any amount of money."

Brianna tried to steady herself and her emotions. It didn't help that Enzo was running in circles and shaking his spill-proof cup so furiously that he was managing to spill it anyway.

"Tell you what," Brianna began in a much softer tone. "Why don't you let me get dressed and we can discuss all this over a cup of coffee."

She indicated Marco with a nod of her head. "He was just leaving."

Mrs. Schelling turned to look at him. Acknowledging Marco for the first time since she'd arrived, she studied him thoroughly. Apparently, she didn't like what she saw. Then she turned her eyes to Brianna's short T-shirt.

"I didn't realize you were entertaining a gentleman," she said with disdain.

Brianna's breath caught. That was probably the worst thing to say in front of her husband. She didn't have a chance to reply. Enzo, who must have sensed the tension between his mama and the nanny, whom he never really took a liking to, walked over and threw his relatively full cup straight at Mrs. Schelling's shin.

"Ow! Do you see?" she cried. "There are plenty of nice, manageable children out there who need looking after. I don't have to put up with—" She gave Enzo a look that could only be described as disgusted. "With this—"

"I am sorry for any trouble my son may have caused," Marco interrupted. His words were cordial enough, but they held a distinct undertone.

"Your son?"

Marco gave her a stiff nod. "Correct. And it just so happens, we no longer need your services. I am here to make alternate arrangements for Enzo."

Marco reached into his back pocket and pulled out a leather wallet. Removing several crisp bills, he extended them to the older woman. Brianna simply stood and stared. She would be hard pressed to match it.

Mrs. Schelling let out another "hmmph" as her pudgy hand closed around the bills. "I dare say I deserve it for all I've had to put up with." She gave Enzo a withering look.

Brianna sighed at the other woman's sourness. "I'm sorry our arrangement didn't work out, Mrs. Schelling. I know Enzo can be a handful, but he's just so young. There's a lot he needs to learn."

Mrs. Schelling pulled her coat tighter as she mumbled something incoherent under her breath. Then she stalked out.

Brianna shut the door and stared at it. What now? Behind her, Marco's sigh was clearly audible.

Brianna turned to him. "Don't you dare say

a word. I don't want to hear anything from you right now."

He gave her a look a teacher might give a child who was having a tantrum.

"Listen," she continued. "I have made no secret of the fact that Enzo has been having some behavior problems since we moved."

"And what of the gentlemen you entertain?"

True to form, Brianna thought. "I do not entertain anyone. Mrs. Schelling just jumped to the wrong conclusion."

Marco's stony glare didn't change.

"In any case, I need to start getting dressed."

"Am I to presume that I will be given the privilege of sitting for my own son?"

"Only if I'm to presume that you'd still like to."

"Of course I do. But I have one question for you first."

She somehow knew that he would. "By all means," she said, not sure how much more conflict she could take in one morning.

"What exactly would you have done if I hadn't shown up?"

There was that hint of accusation in his voice again. "I would have figured something out."

"I'm afraid to guess what that would have been. Were you going to perhaps dump Enzo off on an unprepared neighbor? Or maybe you would have brought him to the restaurant with you where he would have been practically unsupervised."

Oh, he was just too much. "All the neighbors love Enzo, first of all. Secondly, I have a backup sitter."

"And how long would that have taken?"

He had a point. It would probably have taken long enough to make her late again. Enzo's antics had made her late so often in the past, Chef Ansigne had just about lost all patience with her.

"Are you going to sit with him or not?"

"Of course. Don't even pretend you have another option."

Brianna refused to take the bait. "Fine, I'm going to run upstairs and take a shower." She reached down to tussle Enzo's hair. He'd come over to hug her leg, seeking comfort, no doubt.

She leaned over to his eye level. "Enzo, you're going to spend the day with Papa. All right?"

Enzo shook his head and smiled.

Marco immediately went to him. "Why did he

say no?" he asked Brianna. "I thought he remembered who I was."

"He shakes his head when he means yes. He's saying no when he covers his face with his arm."

Marco smiled but it didn't last. "It's been so long, I don't know any of his little quirks."

Here it comes, Brianna thought. Another condemning tirade about how all that was her fault. But instead Marco stroked his son's cheek and started to speak softly to him in Italian. Brianna hadn't forgotten how gentle he could be, how tender.

She shook away the memories. There was no use for them now. Slowly stepping around Marco and Enzo, Brianna silently made her way to the stairway.

Marco heard the water come on upstairs. It would be very hot, he knew. That was how Brianna liked her showers. There would be steam rising off her silky, smooth skin. She was likely using a lavender soap, rubbing it over her curves.

Stop it.

But how? She was no less beautiful than when he'd fallen for her three years ago. It was taking

everything he had not to go up to her now. He
knew she would respond. No matter what had
happened between them and how far they'd been
apart, she was sure to respond. The way she responded to him had never been the problem.

He just wished he understood her.

The nanny's words echoed through his head.
Entertaining a gentleman.

The woman must have witnessed something to
speak as she did. Had she found Brianna "entertaining" in the past?

He clenched his fists.

He had to consider the possibility. Despite
being her husband, he hardly knew Brianna.
When they'd first met on that fateful business trip
to oversee expansion of the family's North Amer-
ican operations, Brianna had still been training
then, barely out of culinary school. One look at
her had triggered an attraction unlike any he'd
ever felt. Nothing he'd ever shared with any other
woman even compared. Maybe that was why he'd
behaved so foolishly that week and then had actually thought they might make it work.

Memories of that first night came back to him.
Marco had made his way to the kitchen just to

get away from all the noise and chaos of a rapidly growing melee. Also to perhaps find something to drink rather than the steady flow of champagne.

He'd nearly run into Brianna as he'd stepped through the door. She'd been a whirlwind of activity, in charge of catering the affair. Somehow, in a white chef's hat and stained apron, she was still breathtakingly striking.

Plus, she'd been so genuine, so real compared to some of the other attendees at that party. He'd been drawn to her immediately. And then when she'd actually ordered him to season appetizers, telling him he may as well make himself useful if he was going to dally in the kitchen.

No one had ever approached him that way.

He'd insisted on taking her out that evening, surprised and relieved when she'd agreed. They'd made arrangements to see each other at least once during his weeklong stay, despite the urgent matters he needed to tend to. Instead, they'd seen each other daily.

Uncharacteristic as it was, he couldn't seem to help himself despite the demands on his sched-

ule. He'd found himself unable to focus on anything but a primitive need to have her.

A need that apparently still possessed him
today.

But after they were married, his responsibilities had often kept him away from home. She was
his wife. She may as well have been a stranger.

When did it change? When did their love affair become a cold battle? She'd told him he spent
too much time working. Too much time away for
his business. She didn't appreciate the pressure
someone in his position faced.

A tug on his leg brought his attention back to
his son.

He crouched down to Enzo's position. "Hey,
little man."

Enzo lifted up his empty cup.

"More juice?"

Enzo shook his head.

"That means yes, right?"

The boy covered his face.

"Well, now I'm confused." Marco stood up
with Enzo cradled in his arms. Setting him on
the couch, he gave the boy a very serious look

then sat next to him. "I believe that was your third nanny in six months, no?"

Enzo gave him a grin that revealed three upper front teeth. Marco started to smile despite himself. He tried to resume the serious expression on his face but gave up when Enzo grabbed a tuft of his hair. The boy had an amazingly strong grip. Pride in his son's strength overrode his pain as Enzo tugged. Hard.

Marco knew he should chastise him but found he couldn't. Too much time had passed since he'd seen his son.

Marco sighed. The sooner they worked out custody, the better. He needed to know he would see Enzo for a few days at least once a month. Anything less would be unbearable.

He and Brianna had no business being married, but their mutual business now was little Enzo. They would have to work to make sure the little boy grew up healthy and happy. It would be difficult, with a mother in New York and a father across the globe in Italy. But it was doable. As soon as Brianna came back from work tonight, he would tell her that. Then he would leave.

CHAPTER THREE

BRIANNA WISHED SHE could crawl back into bed.

In the few short hours since Marco had re-entered her world, it had turned upside down. At work, she'd been flustered, clumsy and distracted.

And she'd been fired. After several warnings, Chef Ansigne had finally relieved her of her position as second line chef. Not that she was surprised. All the incidences of tardiness, then today's repeated mistakes, had sealed her fate. Apparently, lumpy mashed potatoes and droopy salads were Chef Ansigne's breaking points.

And now Brianna had to contend with her soon-to-be ex-husband. Had it only been just this morning he'd shown up at her door? She felt as though she'd lived a whole year since. She let a moment pass on the front porch before inserting her key and entering the house. There was no way she could tell him she'd lost her job.

The sounds of Marco and Enzo playing together resonated through the hallway, Marco's husky voice punctuated by childish squeals of laughter.

She hung up her coat and made her way to the kitchen. The two of them were sitting at the center table, which presently held an array of toys. When Enzo saw her he lifted his arms and yelled, "Mama!"

Brianna went over and gave her son a fierce hug, avoiding eye contact with Marco.

"I thought you weren't going to be home until very late."

She shrugged. "I asked to leave early."

"Hmmm."

Brianna looked up. "What?"

He'd rolled up his sleeves and unbuttoned his collar. His hair was already in disarray, the telltale lock falling forward over his eye. He looked devilish. And incredibly sexy. Her fingers itched to go smooth his hair back, to touch him. She clasped her hands together behind her back.

"Why did you ask to leave early?" he asked.

"Because I didn't want you to feel overwhelmed watching him all by yourself." That was one doozy of a lie. She'd never seen Marco over-whelmed by anything. This was the man who had taken over the family business and doubled it in size. He knew several languages, could seal any deal, and he was an ace boater who won trophies every year.

And somehow he'd ended up married to an orphaned nobody who couldn't keep a job.

"As you can see, we're doing fine," Marco said, then handed Enzo a toy train. "And you're a bad liar, dear wife."

"Don't call me that."

"But that's what you are—my unemployed wife."

The blood drained from her face. How could he know?

"You no longer have a job, do you?"

She swallowed. "Of course I do. There wasn't that much—"

Marco didn't let her finish. "Darling, your chef Ansigne called here. It appears you left your box of knives and tools behind. He'd like you to come get them as soon as possible as he needs the locker for your replacement."

"Fine. I was fired today. Does that make you happy?"

"Of course not. But you don't need to worry about finances."

"That's what you say."

"It's a fact. You're the mother of my child. Technically, you're still my wife."

"I won't be much longer."

"Even so, there's no need to rush. You and Enzo will always be financially secure. I'll see to it."

Of course he would see to it—it meant he could toss her aside with no guilt.

How in the world had she ended up in this predicament? Her career was on the cusp of taking off before she'd gotten pregnant. Apparently, a three-year break could be career suicide.

"Take care of your son, Marco. You have no need to take care of me. I can fend for myself. I always have."

"Ever the independent one."

"In any case, you don't really need to concern yourself," she said, just to spite him. "Seeing as our adventure is over."

"Enzo, why don't you go play with the train track we set up in the other room?" he said, his eyes never leaving hers. The child immediately obeyed. Which was very surprising, for Enzo.

Marco moved around the table and closed the distance between them. Brianna's heart pounded as he approached. Why couldn't she keep her emotions in check when it came to this man?

"As brief as our affair was to be, the fact remains that it resulted in a child." His voice was cold and tight.

"It should have never resulted in marriage."

"I apologize if my wish to legitimize my son put a cramp in your lifestyle."

She sucked in a breath at those words. "What makes you think it did?"

Her regret came too late. The falsehood broke the last of Marco's hold on his temper. In less than a second, he had moved to within inches of where she stood.

"You dare toy with me about such things?" he demanded, his breath hot against her cheek.

To Brianna's horror, her wayward body immediately reacted. A curl of deep, scorching heat erupted in her belly and traveled slowly lower. She wanted to move but seemed unable to. All she could feel was his heat.

"Marco, just stop. I can't fight with you right now," she pleaded, totally depleted of energy all of a sudden. Having him here was wreaking havoc on her senses. A part of her longed for him, had ached to see him and feel him again. But another part, a more logical one, knew better.

That was the part she needed to focus on. It took all of her will to step away. Scooting back around the table, she fought to catch her breath.

Marco stayed where he was. She suspected Enzo's presence in the next room was to thank for that. His breathing was harsh.

"Bree, I don't want to fight either. It's just—"

She held up a hand to stop him from saying any more. "I wish you hadn't shown up here unannounced."

"But I am here."

"Right, to see Enzo. Well, you have. Please leave."

He looked away and shoved his hands into his pockets. "Is that what you really want?"

"Yes," she managed to choke out.

He nodded once. "And what of all the loose ends?"

"Which are?"

His eyes fell on Enzo. "Visitation arrangements."

Of course. "I promise you I'll compromise fully," she said. "I have no interest in keeping him away from you."

He remained silent a moment, his eyes still fixed on his son. "Thank you for that." Then he glanced back at her. "There is also the matter of finances."

"I fully intend to go back to work."

"How? You have no sitter."

"I told you, I have a backup. I've already spoken to him. He can start full-time tomorrow."

Marco's eyebrows shot up just as Brianna realized what she'd said.

"He?" Marco asked.

"Now don't start anything."

"So you have a gentleman friend who watches my son."

She really didn't want to go down this path. No good could possibly come of it. "He's hardly a gentleman friend, Marco. He's a local college student studying elementary education, and he happens to love being around children."

"Who else does he love being around?"

"He's merely a caregiver," Brianna said through

gritted teeth. "A very good one. And he's very dependable. Unlike Mrs. Schelling."

Marco leaned over and gripped the table with both hands.

"Curtis only sits for me."

"I see. Exactly how well do you know him?"

Brianna didn't want to care that he was jumping to all the wrong conclusions. She didn't want to care that he didn't trust her. Why would he? He'd never bothered to know her fully, to know her true character.

One uncharacteristic night of her life, due to a recent breakup, her broken heart had driven her into the arms of a stranger. She'd met Marco only hours earlier, and was in awe of the fact that someone like him actually found her attractive. In a party full of starlets and models, one she was merely attending as the hired help, he'd somehow sought her attention. It took her only hours to fall head over heels in love. And about the same amount of time for her to fall into his bed.

It had been the most intense week of her life. In many ways, she'd been drawn to Marco more than the man she'd been seeing for close to two years before he'd unceremoniously dumped her to pursue a career in Los Angeles.

It had all been so awkward afterward. They were no more than strangers but they'd been intimate. Then, when she'd found out she was carrying their child, it hardly seemed the time to discuss ways to get to know each other better. Not when major decisions had to be made.

"How well, Brianna?" he repeated.

"I know him well enough," she said, suddenly angry. Marco had no power over her. And he had no right to repeatedly judge her so. She noticed his grip on the table tighten.

"Oh, for goodness' sake," she said loudly, then glanced at Enzo. He wasn't used to his mama raising her voice. "Curtis is a very fine young man, just barely in his twenties. There is nothing between us besides an employer-worker relationship."

"You're not out of your twenties yourself."

There was no point in defending herself. It wouldn't work. She shouldn't even need to, not if he truly loved her.

That was laughable. Love had nothing to do with their marriage, not for Marco. He'd just said it himself—it was merely an attempt to legitimize his son.

She smiled, uncaring now that it would inflame his anger. "Nevertheless, I've made my decisions," she said. "I already have some job prospects I can call about. My replacement sitter is lined up. And as soon as you and I work out visitation rights, you can leave."

She was turning to get Enzo when his next words stopped her.

"There's only one problem with all of that."

"And that would be?"

He crossed his arms in front of his chest. "I have no intention of leaving. I'll be here at least the week."

Where had that come from?

Marco watched Brianna's eyebrows rise nearly to her hairline. Well, he was surprised himself at what he'd just said. But it was quite logical really. The woman was a wreck. For goodness' sake, she'd just lost her job, she couldn't hold on to a babysitter and now she was suggesting that Enzo stay in the care of a young man. Brianna needed someone with a strong, sure hand to take care of such issues in a mature, logical manner. Someone like *him*.

The flush on her cheeks and the eyes throwing daggers at him made it clear she thought otherwise. "I didn't realize this was to be an extended stay."

Neither had he. "It just so happens, some business came up that I need to tend to in New York." That was the absolute truth. So what if the "business" he was referring to directly involved her?

"Of course you have business."

"What does that mean?"

"Nothing. Only that I should have realized you would find a way to multitask."

What he wanted was to find a way to keep his son safe. Who exactly was this Curtis to his wife and child? What if Curtis was the type who wanted to just step in and take over another man's life? He would have found an instant family with Brianna and Enzo. The thought had his blood pressure pounding.

"And where do you plan on staying?" Brianna asked.

"Your place is small but there should be enough room."

She gave him a withering look. "My place?"

"That's right. I'll stay here."

She planted her hands on her hips. "Now, why wouldn't you stay at a hotel in Times Square near the Dirici offices?"

"Because Times Square is miles away from Enzo."

"Which would suit me just fine, seeing as he'll be very well taken care of between me and Curtis. If you have such urgent business, you can hardly be expected to spend any time with him."

"I can make time. Especially since I'm in the same city."

She remained silent a moment then lifted her chin. "No."

"No?"

"I said no."

"I beg your pardon."

"I refuse to let you stay here."

He couldn't help his smile. "Afraid to be in such close quarters?"

"I should think that was obvious."

"How about if I promise to behave?"

"You can behave in Times Square."

"Are you saying I should take Enzo with me?"

Brianna's mouth tightened. "Don't even think about it. He stays with me."

"Then I'm not quite sure what we're arguing about. All you have to do is call this male nanny and tell him the offer has been rescinded."

"Absolutely not. I can't do that."

"Why not?" he demanded.

She shook her head very slowly. "I don't want to."

He walked over and picked up the phone. "Fine. I'll do it. What's his number?"

"No, you can't. Listen, you don't understand."

"What is there to understand?"

Her chin quivered. "Curtis needs this. He really needs the position."

"What does that have to do with anything?"

"He needs the job. He just told me today that my offer couldn't have come at a better time. He's experiencing some cash problems and really needs the money."

"Why is any of that my problem?"

She moved over to him and reached for the phone. Marco held on to it. "Please. I would feel awful telling him he won't be getting the funds after all. He told me he couldn't even afford new books for next semester."

"You seem awfully concerned with Curtis's well-being."

Brianna's hand fell to her side. "You wouldn't understand."

Marco understood very well. Curtis sounded like a lovestruck adolescent. Or worse, an opportunist. The young cad was probably pursuing not only his wife but also what little money she had. No doubt he'd connected her last name to the Dirici Foods empire. He was most likely using her generosity and naivety to his utmost advantage. It merely proved Marco's point. Brianna needed his protection. She was clearly easy to manipulate.

There was only one sure way to stop the pup from sniffing around her any longer. "Tell him your husband is back."

"That's not going to help his financial situation," she said a little shakily.

Marco sighed. "How about if I pay him anyway?"

A knowing look appeared in her eyes. "Yet again, that's your solution to everything. Throwing money at it. Well, forget it. He would never accept money for work he didn't do."

Curtis had done quite a number on her. "We'll tell him it's because we're retracting the offer on such short notice."

"He's too proud."

"What a paragon. Did it ever occur to you that you might be being manipulated?"

She glared at him. "You would think that."

He held up the phone. "Just give me his number."

"He truly needs the money, Marco. I told him he had a full-time job."

This was getting quite tiring. "Brianna, I'm not leaving. My son needs me." And so did she.

Brianna nodded and looked down. "This isn't about that."

Oh, hell. "Fine." He slammed the phone down. "Call him later and tell him the job description has changed."

She looked up, searching his face. "What do you mean?"

"Essentially, he's to be on call. I'll ask him to come over if I need to be at the office or if there's a business matter I'm attending to. We'll pay him the same amount because we're asking him to be available at all times during the week. He can either take it or leave it. It's my final offer."

Her shoulders dropped with clear relief and she smiled. "I'm sure he'll take it. He told me he was really desperate for money."

"I'm sure he is."

"I would have felt awful, Marco. I just couldn't tell him he was out of luck again. He said my call was like an answer to a prayer."

A disquieting feeling settled in Marco's chest. Somehow, he'd just agreed to help Brianna's male nanny. This woman made him do the most foolish things. First, making him decide he'd stay, now this. "Yes, well. As long as you understand that I'll be here for a while."

"I understand."

"Good. I'll go see what Enzo's up to."

She stepped in front of him. "Um, I just wanted to—" She halted, looked away again.

"Yes?"

"I mean, it's really hard to not know where your next dollar is coming from. What you did, it was—" She hesitated and returned her gaze to his face. He pondered what she'd just said about not knowing where your next dollar was coming from. Brianna had spent her childhood moving from foster home to foster home after being abandoned by her parents. That much he knew. Though not much more. She didn't particularly like to talk about her past. He could hardly blame her. Sometimes the past was better left behind where it belonged. In that, at least he and Brianna had something in common.

No wonder the marriage had fallen apart.

"What is it, Brianna?"

"I just want to say thanks."

She smiled and he could have sworn he felt warmth in every cell of his body. How childish of him. And he'd accused *her* of being easy to manipulate.

He mumbled a brief response. Then he had to make himself turn away. Before he did something really stupid.

"Really, Marco," she said behind him.

"It's not a big deal, Brianna."

"Curtis would disagree."

"I couldn't care less what your Curtis thinks."

"I'm just trying to say that he'd appreciate it, that's all. And I appreciate it too."

He turned to tell her the truth, to just admit it. He'd relented because of her.

But something else entirely came out of his

mouth. "You know exactly how to get your way, don't you?"

"What?" Brianna looked at him in bafflement. "What is that supposed to mean?"

"A flick of the lashes. A flirtatious look here and there. And I did exactly what you wanted. Your precious Curtis still has a job. And you've still got your feminine wiles. Let's just move on now, shall we?"

She slammed her hands on her hips. "Why? Why did I think you were capable of any decency? You're still exactly the same, aren't you? Nothing's changed."

"Apparently not."

"For the briefest moment back then I thought perhaps you might have grown a little. What a fool I can be."

"Then we have something in common, after all."

"Hah," she barked. "We don't have a thing in common."

"Are you finished? I believe Enzo may be ready for bed."

Brianna threw her hands up. "Yes. I believe we're done."

She stomped toward Enzo and picked him up.

"I'll be upstairs giving Enzo his bath," she said. "After that, I'm going to bed."

"I'll help you."

She whirled around.

Marco rolled his eyes. "With Enzo's bath, I meant."

She glared at him. "You'll find the spare room upstairs. I don't even want to know you're here for the next week. Do you understand?"

Now that, Marco thought, watching her go up the stairs, would be easier said than done.

CHAPTER FOUR

COFFEE. SOMEONE HAD definitely brewed coffee.
There was a ray of light streaming through the
small crack of the blind on her bedroom window.
The bright sun outside told her it was later than
her usual wake-up time. Much later. And there
was something else. It was quiet. Way too quiet.
She fumbled around for the digital clock. It was
almost eight.

Brianna jolted upright and climbed out of bed.
Something wasn't right. Enzo never slept this late.

Panic clenched at her chest as she hastened her
way to his nursery. Gripping the door handle, she
braced herself for all the possible horrors that
might explain why Enzo hadn't woken yet. Was
he ill? Had he hurt himself somehow?

Could Marco have taken—

No. He wouldn't.

When she finally found herself next to the little
crib, the rush of relief brought tears to her eyes.

Enzo was sleeping soundly, his chubby fingers closed around the silk trimming of his favorite blankie. She watched as his eyelids fluttered, then sealed closed again. Brianna couldn't help reaching for him. At the risk of waking him, she touched his cheek, stroked her fingers through the fine baby curls on his head. He looked so peaceful.

So vulnerable.

"He just fell asleep again."

She jumped at the quiet voice behind her. It was Marco, on the rocking chair in the corner of the room. He stood and motioned for her to follow him out into the hallway.

"He woke up at six," Marco said when they were outside. "I read to him for a while then rocked him back to sleep."

"I didn't hear him," Brianna said.

"I'm a lighter sleeper. Always have been. Besides, I know you were pretty tired."

"Well, thank you."

"There's no need to thank me for putting my own son back to sleep."

Brianna had to refrain from grunting. How many nights had Marco tucked Enzo in when he was an infant? "I just meant it allowed me to sleep in, that's all. Have you always been this hard to thank?"

He gave her that insolent stare again. The look that made Brianna feel as if he were actually touching her. "Too bad we're splitting up. I could come up with all sorts of ways you could thank me."

His words sent heat shooting through her core. At least she was better prepared this time. Unlike yesterday's thin T-shirt, last night she'd worn bulky flannel pajamas to bed. But somehow, she still felt naked to his gaze.

Marco was already dressed in casual khaki pants and a black silk shirt that brought out the hue of his eyes. He honestly had to be the most handsome man she'd ever met. All the more reason she wasn't about to touch his last comment with a ten-foot pole.

"Are you going somewhere?" she asked, changing the subject.

"I was waiting for you to wake up. I'm going to spend the morning at Dirici's. I'll go through some paperwork then talk to the managers as they come in."

She nodded. Same old Marco. His second

morning here and already he couldn't wait to rush into the Dirici offices. "I see. If you don't mind my saying, that all sounds very routine. What about the 'pressing' business matter that had you altering your travel plans yesterday?"

He frowned. "I'm tending to it."

"Well, I hope it's taken care of very soon."

A shadow passed over his face. She couldn't make out what it meant.

"Will you be here all day?" he asked.

She sighed. She certainly had nothing else to do. There was no longer a job to prep recipes for. And she'd already contacted all the possible leads she knew of about a new position. A cook's position at a decent restaurant wasn't exactly a job you scanned the want ads for. An opening such as that would be more a word-of-mouth opportunity.

"I might take Enzo down to the park for a couple of hours. I don't want to be away from the house too long though, in case any of the job possibilities pan out."

Marco's lips tightened. "You wouldn't want to miss that," he said dryly.

"Is there a reason for sarcasm this early?"

"I have to go," he said, ignoring her question and leaving the room. "I left all my numbers on the table for you. My New York assistant's name and number is there too."

Moments later Brianna heard the front door shut. Her mornings were usually hectic and stressful, with getting Enzo ready and preparing for her workday. This morning Enzo was sleeping soundly and she had nothing to do but wait for him. It was almost as if Marco's arrival had added an element of calm to her life.

Right. That was ridiculous. Calm and Marco Dirici were not words to be used in the same sentence. Ever.

The events of the last evening fluttered through her mind as she went downstairs to pour herself a cup of coffee. Her anger flared in response. The nerve of that man. She had been so surprised at the offer he'd been willing to extend to Curtis. Marco wasn't terribly flexible by nature. For a brief instant she had deluded herself that he may have a heart.

But then he'd turned on her. Which made no sense at all. She'd simply been trying to thank him. Marco had to care a little about her feelings to have made the offer he did.

Or so she'd thought. Until he had turned surly and accusatory again.

She gulped down several swigs, not even bothering to season it with her usual packet of raw sugar.

What did it matter anyhow? It wasn't as if she had to bother trying to figure out Marco or his mood swings any longer. She'd spent enough time over the last three years trying to do that. Every time he went away on an extended business trip with barely a goodbye, she had tried to determine what she might have done to upset him. Or the times he returned and retired to his own suite with barely a nod in her direction.

She slammed her mug down on the table. The few times he had spoken to her it had been to issue an ultimatum or question her about this or that. Where had she been? Who had she seen?

My attempt to legitimize my son.

His words shouted through her mind. That was how he'd referred to their marriage. And even though she'd known that was all their union had been about, the way he'd said it so casually had sliced through her heart.

The shrill ring of the kitchen phone broke into her thoughts. She hadn't even had half a cup yet, wasn't really awake enough to talk to anyone. But she had to answer it before it woke Enzo.

"Hello," she said.

"Brianna Dirici, please." Brianna gripped the phone tighter. She recognized the deep accent immediately. And it was as welcome as ice cream on a hot day.

"This is she."

"Ms. Dirici. This is Chef Ziyad of the Ruby Room on the Upper East Side. I'm calling regarding your expressed interest in a cook's position."

Of all the places she'd applied to, this one was her top choice. The Ruby Room attracted the kind of clientele every chef longed to cook for. Dare she hope?

"Yes?"

"I imagine you are still in the market for a position?"

Was she ever. "That's correct."

"Ms. Dirici, we might have an opportunity for you."

Yes! "Please, call me Brianna."

"Very well then. Brianna. Your reputation indicates a specialty with ethnic mix cuisine."

"It's what I've spent the bulk of my career working on, Chef Ziyad. Spanish tapas for the most part."

"And I understand you're quite skilled with puff pastry."

"Mainly Mediterranean appetizers."

"Well, we attract quite a number of international diners. And I'm looking to expand our mezze menu. Would you be able to come in and discuss all this?"

Brianna cleared her throat. It wasn't wise to sound too desperate. Never mind that she was actually jumping up and down in her kitchen. "Whenever you'd like, Chef Ziyad."

"Excellent. I'll give you my assistant's information. Please call him and set up a time." Brianna took down the information and hung up. A huge grin settled on her face. She'd done it! And it had taken less than a day.

"So there, Josef Ansigne," she said aloud. "Who needs you?"

Her gaze fell to the piece of paper Marco had left with his numbers on it. She walked over and picked it up. He'd indicated that his cell phone would be the best number to call first. She ran her finger over his writing, outlining his sharp, bold strokes.

If theirs was a real marriage, her husband would be the first person she'd call to celebrate the good news. She couldn't help but imagine how good it would feel to have Marco say he was happy for her. That he was proud of her.

She put the slip of paper back down.

It wasn't a real marriage. And Marco wanted nothing more from her than for her to live in Italy and care for their son while he himself went about his own life. Far from celebrating such news, Marco would be upset about the development.

She should have her head examined for having such fantasies. The time for hoping for anything meaningful with Marco was over. All she had to do where he was concerned was get through the next few days until he finished whatever he had to do. Then he could go back to Italy. Then they could get their divorce.

Somehow the utter giddiness of just a few short seconds ago had fallen away completely. She glanced at the clock above the oven. Nine o'clock. Enzo had slept in long enough. If she didn't go wake him now, his whole schedule for the day would be off. By evening she'd have a cranky, sore little tyrant on her hands.

She started up the stairs to go get him. Any further celebrating would have to wait.

Marco continued to stare at the column of numbers in front of him. The same column of numbers on the same screen he'd been staring at for the last fifteen minutes. Finally, in disgust he pushed his chair away from the desk and swiveled around to stare out his floor-to-ceiling office window at the traffic outside. Forty-Fifth Street was fully alive. Pedestrians were out in droves cutting through rows of stationary cars.

For someone who prided himself on his concentration skills, Marco certainly didn't feel focused today. He'd wasted the better part of an hour accomplishing next to nothing.

He rested his head back and stared at the sky. The sun had abandoned it hours ago. Thick rolling clouds littered the horizon. A faint haze of drizzle curtained the atmosphere.

All in all, the day had changed to match his mood completely.

What in the world was he doing here? Nothing in the paperwork or the operations needed immediate attention. If anything, his managers were going to great lengths to pretend he wasn't in the way. His unexpected visit had cut into various meetings and several executives' schedules. He was merely hampering business.

That made him angry. That reminded him of the reason he was in New York in the first place. Brianna.

The woman was a thorn in his side. The plan had been so simple. Go to New York. Check on Enzo. Come to a fair agreement regarding his son and all the other loose ends that unraveled at the end of a marriage. It all brought him back to the same question. Why was he still in New York?

Because he was a jealous, mindless fool. Over a woman who was never really his. If he witnessed one of his friends in the same situation, he knew exactly what he'd do.

The phone rang and he snatched it to his ear. "Marco Dirici."

"I know who you are. At least I think I do."

His grandmother. A smile tugged at his mouth. "Hello, Nonna."

"I'm your nonna in name only, I see so little of you."

"You usually can't wait to get rid of me."

"You know that is absolutely not true."

"There are times I wonder."

She snorted. "How is our little *bambino*, eh? I've so missed him."

At the mention of his son, warmth spread through Marco's chest. "He's wonderful, Nonna. You should see how he's grown in the months since we've seen him."

What followed was a virtual quiz. Nonna asked him about everything from Enzo's diet to his toilet habits. Then she hesitated. When she spoke again, Marco immediately sensed unease in her voice. "How are things there, Marco?" she asked.

He sighed. "You mean with Brianna."

"The house just isn't the same without her."

He picked up a pen, tapped it against the desk, then dropped it. "Our separation was for the best."

"You can be so sure?"

"Nonna, I don't have time for this."

"You don't have time for your grandmother? Of course not, Mr. Hot Shot Businessman. Why would you want to speak to a silly, feeble old woman?"

That comment was downright laughable. His grandmother was about as feeble as an army general. "Nonna, that won't work. You're not going to guilt me into talking to you about this."

"Fine." Nonna's voice was brusque. "But I won't let you hang up without giving you some hard-learned advice."

Marco sighed. Nonna had made it clear before he left that his only goal on this trip should be to bring his wife and son back. She had no idea how irreparable things had gotten between him and Brianna. This was so not the time to try and explain it to her. "Unwanted advice would be more accurate."

"I don't know what went wrong between you and that lovely bride of yours. But you should do everything in your power to rectify it." She paused, as if considering whether to add her next comment. Marco wished she hadn't. "I saw the way you looked at each other, son. Surely there's still affection between you two."

Marco did not want to get into this. And certainly not with the woman who'd raised him. He'd rather walk through hot coals. What Nonna had interpreted as affection was nothing more than a fierce physical attraction that had struck him nearly blind with wanting when he'd first met Brianna. An attraction that had resulted in a child the very first time they'd been together.

He was trying to come up with yet another tactful way to say "none of your business" when Nonna continued. "That child, my great-grandson, I only have his best interests at heart. I care more for that boy than—"

"Nonna." He cut her off, and this time the warning was clear in his voice.

She wouldn't be intimidated. No surprise there. "You listen to me, young man." Marco had no doubt she was shaking her finger at the phone. "That child needs to feel secure, he needs to sense that he's completely protected. It's so important for the stage he's in."

Marco closed his eyes and pinched the bridge of his nose. "That's why I'm here, Nonna. To make sure he knows I'll always be there for him." And to make sure that Brianna knew that as well.

"I mean now, Marco. Presently, when all these decisions are being made."

Enough was enough. "Nonna, I love you, but you really don't need to concern yourself with this." As in, *it's really none of your business.* A concept older Italian grandmothers didn't seem to understand.

"Of course I do, I love that boy. You and Brianna are pulling his world apart. Do everything you can to give him any sense of comfort possible. Or the consequences…"

Marco straightened in his chair. As much as he was trying to resist, he somehow couldn't help taking the bait. "What do you suggest?"

"Ay, ay, ay," Nonna said, as if he was missing something very obvious. "Bring them home. You have given up on your wife much too easily. Why will you not fight? Until the two of you figure it all out?"

"Nonna, I'm not going to beg a woman to stay when she doesn't want to. We both know the humiliation in that."

Silence. Then he heard a deep sigh on the other end of the line. "Listen," she began. "Brianna is nothing like the woman you try to compare her to."

Marco's fingers tightened around the receiver. He had to bite his tongue against the reply he wanted to blurt out. She *was* still his grandmother. "Brianna's made her decision. I will honor it."

He heard a disagreeing grunt from the other end of the line. The woman was persistent. "You're wrong about that. You need to tell her, Marco. But first you need to see it."

By the time he hung up, Marco felt as if he'd sailed an hour through a turbulent storm. His grandmother's words replayed in his head. Particularly her warnings about Enzo and his need for stability at this stage.

But Marco was truly at a loss. How much more

could he do? The whole reason for this trip was to make sure he remained a steady and solid part of the boy's life. As far as his wife was concerned, that was a whole different story. Nonna was the one who was wrong. It was way too late to try and work things out with Brianna.

CHAPTER FIVE

A BRISK AUTUMN breeze rustled the trees and nipped at Marco's face as he made his way toward the gazebo in the middle of Memorial Park. According to the note she'd stuck on the door, Brianna had taken Enzo here to play.

It was late afternoon and Marco found himself enjoying the fresh air. The brief walk from Brianna's house had started to work out the kinks in his joints garnered from an unproductive, frustrating morning at the office.

Surprising as it was, he was looking forward to spending time in the kiddie park with his son and his...well, Brianna. He had to stop thinking of her in terms of being his wife.

Marco's stride faltered. She was only that in the most literal sense of the word. And wouldn't be for much longer. Just cold, hard fact. They both needed to move on.

He heard them before he spotted them. Brianna's punctuating laughter mixed in with a small boy's giggles. They were under a large oak near the gazebo. Brianna had her arms spread wide, twirling around in circles. Enzo ran madly around her. He stopped, bent to grab an armful of dry leaves, then threw them at his mother. Brianna laughed harder.

Almost everyone else in the park stared at the spectacle. A couple of women were smiling. Several other ladies looked to be snickering to each other behind cupped hands. A few merely stared as if they thought her mad.

Marco knew Brianna wouldn't care about any of that.

She looked like a gypsy. A crimson-red band wrapped around her head did a very poor job of containing her long tangle of curls. A fitted black sweater hugged her hips and stopped midthigh. Beneath it, her long, shapely legs were clad in black leggings. On her feet were trendy chunky-heeled shoes, the ones that arched the foot in that sexy way that made a man want to tear them off and run his hands up her legs.

She was so different from the women he'd dated before her. Those ladies wouldn't have been caught dead letting themselves be covered with leaves. Even a trip to the park would entail the utmost preparation and wardrobe prep. Not that many of them would venture to a park to begin with. Compared to his previous paramours, his wife was downright Bohemian. Before he'd met her, Marco would have never guessed just how attractive he found it.

None of his previous relationships had even come close to becoming serious. Which had suited him just fine, he'd liked it that way. But then he'd met Brianna. Her earthiness, her sheer zest for life called to him like no one else ever had.

And the way she treated their son. At times like this it took his breath away. Memories assaulted him. He wasn't much older than Enzo when his own mother had packed up and left the first time.

He would do anything to spare his own child that level of pain.

He made himself tear his gaze away. The only other man in the park had his eyes set firmly on Brianna; his look was clearly appreciative. Marco cleared his throat and scowled at him when the man finally managed to look his way.

Brianna noticed him as well. His eyes met hers and the laughter immediately stopped. She stopped the twirling and bent down to brush leaves off Enzo's hair.

Marco jammed his hands in his pockets. There was no reason to treat him like a killjoy ogre. The pleasant greeting he'd been ready to approach her with died on his lips.

"We didn't think we'd see you so soon," Brianna said, lowering herself onto the blanket behind them. She didn't sound very happy about it.

"Disappointed?" Marco asked as he picked Enzo up and tousled his hair.

The blush on her cheeks deepened. "Surprised."

"Why is that?"

She shrugged. "I just figured you'd be at the office all day. In Italy, you never returned home until late. Sometimes very late."

He turned to look at her as he set down his squirming son. She had her hands wrapped around an insulated cup. Her gaze was fixed on Enzo as he moved to the sandbox a few feet away.

"If you weren't expecting me," he continued, "why did you leave a note?"

She took a small sip and he had to force himself

not to watch her lips. "That note was for Curtis. He said he might stop by. You know, to go over what we expect of him over the next few days."

Curtis. Marco felt a cold chill slither over his skin. She'd been expecting to meet Curtis here. This quaint scene before him. His wife. His son. It was all meant to be shared with someone else, with another man.

He stood abruptly. The note he still held seemed to burn his palm. He crumpled it up and stuck it in his pocket.

"Sorry to disappoint you."

She blinked at him. "I expected you to work late and left a note for Curtis because he said he might come by before we left. I fail to see why that compels you to snap at me."

He gritted his teeth. "I was merely apologizing, *cara*. That I showed up rather than your so-called nanny."

Brianna drew back. Then stood as well and reached for Enzo's hand. "Let's go, baby."

"Are we leaving?"

"It's time for his nap. So yes, Enzo and I are leaving." She placed the child gently in his stroller then buckled him in. "You are more than welcome to stay. Maybe the fresh air will clear your head."

With that she brushed past him, pushing the stroller in front of her. Marco had to step out of the way to avoid having his toes run over. Taking a deep, calming breath, he turned and followed them out of the park.

The image of her laughing and playing with Enzo from just a few moments ago had completely evaporated. Why had he ever thought he could be part of such an image in the first place?

Her fingers were tingling. Brianna looked down at her knuckles and realized she couldn't possibly grip the stroller handle any tighter. By the time the three of them made it to the wooden gate in front of her house, she was as red-hot mad as an oiled skillet. The brisk walk in the strong autumn wind had done nothing to douse her ire. She was grateful for that. She needed the anger, welcomed it. Because if she let go of being mad, she knew she would have to acknowledge how deeply he could hurt her.

She pushed Enzo's stroller into the front yard and gently lifted him. The afternoon of play followed by the short stroll back had put him to sleep. Without a word to Marco, she carried Enzo up the porch steps and into the house.

She longed to slam the door behind her, right in Marco's face, but didn't dare with the sleeping child cradled in her arms.

She'd had enough. She managed to change Enzo without waking him and settled him in his crib for what she hoped would be a long nap. Then she stormed into her own room without bothering to go back downstairs where *he* was.

This was the reason she had left Italy. This was why she and Marco had to be apart. Marco had nothing but disdain for her. She was far too unrefined for him. Too impulsive.

Too common.

It was a wonder he'd ever wanted to marry her in the first place. Though that decision had nothing to do with her and everything to do with his traditional values and culture. He simply wanted to claim his child. This whole sham of a marriage was her fault. She'd known his true motivations.

Someone like Brianna Stedman should have known better. For heaven's sake, his proposal had been made over a very tense lunch one afternoon after she'd called him to tell him about the pregnancy. He'd flown back the next day. She hadn't been able to eat a thing on her plate, and it had nothing to do with morning sickness.

No, it was all because every cell within her was screaming that this was all wrong. The man across her at the quaint restaurant table was merely doing what he thought was the responsible thing. Love or emotion played no variable in the equation. Marco had even listed all the reasons their marriage would make sense, as if reading off some document in bullet form. He was approaching it as practically as another business deal.

She'd known all that and had said yes anyway. Foolish as it was.

In her blind desire to finally become part of a family, she'd rushed into a marriage for all the wrong reasons, hoping it would somehow all work out. Like some kind of Cinderella story. Well, real life went hardly the way of fairy tales.

Stomping toward the bathroom, she peeled off her clothes and stepped into the shower. It took a while but the pulsing, steamy water slowly started to ebb the edge off her emotions.

She shut the water off and wrapped a towel around herself.

Marco was waiting for her outside the bathroom door.

Brianna pulled the towel tighter. "I'm not dressed."

He turned his back and crossed his arms in front of his chest.

Exasperated, but too tired to tell him to leave, Brianna went to her closet and retrieved her long thick robe. Yanking it on and tying it around her, she let the towel drop.

Marco chose that moment to turn back and watched the towel fall to the floor. He looked at her with clouded eyes. Despite the bulky terry robe, Brianna felt naked and exposed under his gaze.

She pushed past that thought and grabbed at the anger again. "Listen, Marco. This arrangement is not going to work at all if you keep behaving the way you have been."

"How exactly would that be?"

"You have to give me room and you have to give me leeway. I'm simply trying to move the best I can."

He merely nodded. A surge of relief spiked

through her that he wasn't going to argue. So she went on.

"It's something I need to do. For my son. And yes, also for myself."

"Very well, *cara*." Marco spoke with all seriousness after several moments of silence. "Your point is made."

For the next few days, Marco seemed to do his best to heed Brianna's wishes. He was polite, considerate and genteel. She hardly recognized him. During the day, he went to his office. In the evening, he spent hours with Enzo either reading to him or playing on the floor. A foolish part of her would even be sorry to see him leave. He was due to depart in the morning.

He seemed to be a completely different man from the one she had lived with in Italy. And watching him with her son was doing near damage to her psyche. If she wasn't careful, she could easily fall for the man. Again. She had to remind herself this wasn't the real Marco. Here in New York he was in a different setting, a whole different atmosphere. Upon his return to Italy, Brianna had no doubt he would turn into the hardcore, determined businessman who spent most of his hours running a global conglomerate.

She couldn't harbor any pretense that the Marco she was currently observing was the true personality of the man.

It was the reason she had to make sure to maintain her emotional bearings and move on. She had to make her own way, find her own direction. Growing up being bounced from one foster home to the next. Making a name for herself in her chosen field would mean the world to her.

That was why it was so frustrating that she'd been unable to get hold of Chef Ziyad's assistant. After several attempts and messages, the man still hadn't returned her calls.

Brianna sighed and picked up the phone once more to give it yet another try. Again, she got voice mail. Fighting the urge to slam the receiver back in its cradle, she bit back the surge of disappointment. She had to acknowledge that perhaps Ziyad's offer had occurred on an impulsive whim. The man was notoriously spacy and temperamental.

It was quite likely that, as far as her career

was concerned, she may very well be back at square one.

Here she was, no real career prospects and a marriage in shambles. Failure at every turn. As far as orphan tales went, hers was clearly not to be a success story.

CHAPTER SIX

IT WAS PAST two in the morning when Marco heard the first shriek. He felt the next one as much as he heard it. A jolt of alarm shot through him. Enzo.

Marco sprinted to the nursery. Brianna was already there, lifting the baby out of his crib.

Marco watched helplessly as she tried to soothe him, rocking him back and forth, whispering into his ear. It was all to no avail. The scene made Marco's blood run cold. Something was terribly wrong with his child.

Brianna lifted her eyes and found his. Even in the dim light afforded by the small night-light, he could see the alarm in her face. Enzo was wailing frantically now, flailing his arms. Marco noticed she was having trouble holding on to him.

"Here, let me have him."

Brianna hesitated. Then she carefully handed

him over. Enzo didn't seem to notice he'd switched hands. His screams continued.

"It's okay, little man," Marco whispered in his ear. "I'm here. Just calm down. All right, son, just calm down."

Enzo wasn't having any of it. He started pumping his legs furiously, his screams becoming louder. Brianna seemed in a near panic now.

"It's all right," Marco said in his gentlest voice, not sure if he was addressing her or his son. "Everything's fine, love."

He nuzzled Enzo's ear, whispering the same phrase repeatedly. He lost count how many times he said it.

"Son, I want you to calm down. It's all right. Papa's here."

The ticking of the cartoon character wall clock seemed to echo throughout the room between the screams. Shadows moved across the opposite wall as a car drove down the street outside. Enzo continued to yell, his tiny fists clenched tight.

He could do nothing but pace with his child in his arms. At some point, his words turned to Italian. He hadn't even realized he'd switched over. Maybe it made a difference because Enzo's wails gradually grew quieter. Eventually, they went from shriek-like screams to sad, woeful moaning.

Finally, Marco saw him open his eyes wide. He focused for a full moment on his father's face. Then suddenly, he threw his arms around Marco's neck. Marco rubbed the tiny back, still whispering in Italian. Enzo tightened his arms around his father's neck. His little legs slowed their jerky thrusts. The tiny arms around him loosened their hold but remained tight around his neck.

Marco was afraid to move, afraid any change would resume the screaming. So he just stood there, dropping the barest of kisses on the top of Enzo's head.

He finally looked up to Brianna. Some of the color had returned to her face. She still looked shell-shocked. Marco took the risk of shifting Enzo ever so slightly to reach for her. He gently ran the back of his fingers down Brianna's cheek then gave her what he hoped was a reassuring smile.

She bit her lip and felt Enzo's forehead. At her touch, Enzo's wails stopped completely.

Several moments later, once Enzo's breathing had gone from sharp short bursts to the long sighs of a child in deep slumber, Marco slowly, gently placed him back in his crib. He stared at him a moment. Enzo looked completely peaceful, if not a little exhausted. Marco stepped aside as Brianna covered him up. She placed a plush teddy bear to his cheek, which Enzo immediately grabbed.

For a while, they both just stood and watched him. He had no idea how much time had actually gone by. When Marco was certain Enzo had settled for good, he guided Brianna by her elbow to the door.

Out in the hall, he turned the hall light on and rubbed a weary hand down his face. Brianna was trembling.

"Hey, try and get a hold of yourself, Bree. He's fine now."

She nodded. "I've never seen him like that." She looked up at him, her eyes full of fear. He wanted to go to her, to pull her into his arms. Soothe her with gentle words and soft kisses, the way he had with Enzo in there.

He crossed his arms before he could reach for her. "So he's never done that before?"

She shook her head vehemently. "No, not even

close. He wakes up all the time during the middle of the night but usually acts like he just wants to play."

"He must have had nightmares before."

"Of course. But nothing to even make note of. He awakens, I rock him back to sleep and that's the extent of it. What he did just now—" She hugged her arms around herself. Marco couldn't help reaching over this time, he just couldn't. She looked so frightened, much like a child herself. He gave her shoulder a small squeeze and quickly tried to pull his hand away. But she grabbed it, held on to his fingers as if he was pulling her out of treacherous waters.

"Do you think it's us, Marco?"

He gave a weary sigh. "Perhaps. My being here may have triggered memories of his old life."

She'd finally voiced the thought he was certain they'd both feared. Marco ran his hands through his hair. "*Cara*, I just don't know. We don't let him see us argue, but I daresay he's sharp enough to sense the tension between us."

Brianna threw her hands up. "But he's never acted like this. We're not doing anything all that different than the way we were in Italy."

"Old habits die hard," he said dryly.

"Maybe he's just older now and it affects him more."

Marco let out a deep breath; perhaps he'd been holding it since he'd heard the first scream. His eyes stung from tiredness and he rubbed them until they hurt. "Looks like you were right. My being here has had a negative effect on him."

Brianna stepped to him and touched his arm. "No, please don't think that. He's been so happy these past few days every time he sees you. His behavior has greatly improved."

Marco couldn't believe she was trying to comfort him. About this of all things. He looked down where her fingers lay on his bare skin then looked back into her eyes.

"No, if anything, it was me," she continued. "I've put him through too many changes. Just the turnover of our nannies has led to too many adjustments for someone so small. He must feel so helpless, while all these decisions are made around him."

The words were almost an exact echo of Nonna's earlier. He hated it when the old woman made sense.

Brianna searched his face. "What is it? What are you thinking?"

"We've both been neglectful of his needs, Brianna. We didn't give him enough credit because he was so young."

"I guess neither one of us saw how intuitive he is."

He looked up at the ceiling. "The only one who did was Nonna."

"How do you mean?"

"I spoke to her that first day after I arrived. At the office. She was very concerned about the effect all of our maneuverings were having on Enzo. I didn't want to give her concerns much thought."

"What exactly did she say?"

"Something quite close to what you just did. That all sorts of decisions are being made around him and he's probably confused." He shrugged. "Frightened."

"She's right. She saw it better than we did. Did she say it was my fault?"

"Brianna, she doesn't think that."

"Do you?" she asked, her lips giving an almost imperceptible tremble.

"Of course not."

She looked far from convinced.

Marco sighed. "Listen, we both neglected to gauge his response properly to our splitting up. We just need to be more careful."

"What else did Marie say?" she asked.

"It doesn't matter."

"There's something you're not telling me, Marco. I can see it."

He shrugged. "You're not going to like it."

Brianna rolled her eyes. "I don't like any of this."

"That he needs to be in more familiar surroundings, near familiar people, during all these changes."

She narrowed her eyes. "Like the villa he was born in and great-grandmother who doted on him and the staff he's known since he was merely days old."

Marco nodded. "She thinks it would be better for Enzo if the two of you were back in Italy while we finalize what to do about the end of our marriage."

Brianna moved away from him and paced the small hallway. She didn't say a word for several moments, just moved up and down from the door to her room back to where Marco stood.

He had known she wouldn't like what Nonna suggested. It was, after all, the very thing Brianna wanted to be done with; their life together in Italy. But right now, he couldn't read her at all. All she did was pace.

Finally, he couldn't stand it any longer.

"Bree, I'm sorry. But I'm tired and will be travelling most of the day tomorrow. I should at least pretend to sleep."

She halted and turned to him. "You can't be apart from Enzo now. It would only upset him all the more after having you for only a few days."

That set him back a step. "But you said you wanted me to leave, vehemently. Several times."

She bit her lip. "I do. You can't stay here."

"Brianna, what exactly is it that you do want?"

She shook her head. "I'm not sure I know anymore."

Marco waited.

"Nonna's right," she finally said.

"What exactly do you think she's right about?"

"About all of it."

"All of it?"

She looked over to Enzo's door. "I can't risk damaging my son. I just can't risk it. I don't know what we should do in the long run. I just know I never want to see him that upset again."

Marco blinked. "Let me make sure I understand. You're willing to return to Italy."

She pulled back her hair. "I guess we have to. Between his behavior issues and what he did just now..." Her voice faltered, as if reliving it.

"For how long?"

"I don't know exactly. A week perhaps. Maybe a month. I guess we'll have to reevaluate everything as Enzo improves."

"I see," Marco said. "What about what you were trying to do here?"

The lip quiver again. But then she raised her chin. "It can all wait until I'm sure Enzo's all right. If I have to, I can give up the house. My landlord would love to let me out of the lease. The housing market has gotten tighter since I moved in, he can make much more renting to a new tenant."

"I see," Marco said. "And I suppose it's as convenient a time as any, given that you're no longer employed."

Something flooded her eyes before she quickly looked away. "Right," she said. "Can you postpone your return flight a day or two? There are things I need to wrap up here."

"Of course. And I'll let Nonna know to expect all of us. She'll be thrilled."

Brianna looked back up to study him. "Please make sure she understands. This is nothing more than an extended visit. To make sure Enzo's all right."

Marco nodded, suddenly feeling exhausted. "I'll explain it, *cara*."

"And you understand that too, don't you?"

He stared at her. "You mean I shouldn't entertain any notions that you're doing this for any other reason than for Enzo."

"Well, yes."

"Don't worry. I know you can't wait to be rid of the husband you no longer want to be with. I won't forget that."

"That's not what I said. I just feel that you and I should focus on how to move on as individuals, despite this temporary setback."

He came close to telling her to forget it, this whole situation was impossible. And now she was essentially telling him not to get his hopes up. With a firm grip on his anger, he forced himself to give her a careless smile.

"What makes you think I haven't moved on?" he asked. "And that this isn't a setback for me to suddenly have my wife back in residence."

His wife. She was that in the legal sense certainly. But something had happened to sever the initial connection they'd shared. An undeniable fact. Around the time right before Enzo's birth. Her health scares during pregnancy were more stressful than he would have cared to admit. Coupled with the frustration of not being able to touch her, the tenuous bond they'd been building had suffered an unrecoverable blow. Tenuous it must have been indeed.

Brianna seemed to mull over his statement as she chewed her lip.

"Don't worry that I'll misunderstand, Bree," he said. "You're returning to our home. I have no expectation that you'll return to our bed."

Brianna crossed the note to call Curtis off her to-do list. She'd apologized profusely and made him accept his would-be salary because of all the unexpected changes to the original offer.

She looked around at the tidy colonial house she'd called home for the past six months. Everything had been packed up hastily and the windows were all sealed. Though they'd been comfortable here, she'd be hard pressed to say she would miss it. For all she knew, it had been the mistake of her life, coming here to New York. Had she in fact caused serious damage to the psyche of her son? Had all of his behavioral issues been the result of her leaving Italy and all that he'd known?

She shuddered at the thought. If true, it would be something she'd never forgive herself for.

Going back was the right thing for little Enzo. Oh, but she knew it was the wrong thing for her. The last thing she needed was to be back in Marco's home. Marco's romantic villa had been the ultimate location for an impromptu honeymoon. Set amongst the lush, high hills outside of Positano, the Mediterranean-style house had taken Brianna's breath away when she'd first seen it.

While she'd been passed from one location to another during childhood, her husband had been born and grown up in a mansion his ancestors had built and maintained. On land his forbearers had cultivated.

And Marco was the true master of his ancestral home. He'd taken her through every room and given her a detailed history of the structure and the lands on which it had stood for close to a hundred years. He'd kissed her on the veranda overlooking the sea. That was one of the last good memories she had of living there. Before everything had gone sour.

Dear heavens, how would she cope being back there and the sure damage it would cause to her heart?

But staying here was definitely not worth the risk. Not when it came to her son. And after all, it wasn't like she really had much of a life here at this point. She'd lost one job and another one she thought had opened up turned out not to bear out. There hadn't been much time to make any new friends. All her old ones were busy with their own lives with focuses on career advancement and social activities. They no longer had much in common with the mother of a temperamental toddler.

It was time to return to Italy. She would have to re-evaluate her life once she got there. All that mattered now was her little boy and his well-being.

Even in a private jet, it was not easy to travel with a small child. Marco pulled Enzo onto his lap for what seemed like the hundredth time. The boy apparently had made a game of it to crawl from his mother's lap to Marco's over and over again. Marco wasn't sure how he'd handle the hours on the flight if Enzo kept it up.

"Isn't there anything in there that might keep him occupied?" Marco asked, pointing to the canvas bag full of toys Brianna had carried onto the plane.

Brianna blew a strand of hair off her face. "He seems not to be interested in playing with toys."

He wrestled with Enzo as the child tried to settle himself just right. "Couldn't you have brought along things he enjoyed?"

Brianna's eyes widened. "Why, Marco. I hadn't thought of that. What an excellent source of child-rearing logic you are."

Her sarcasm was so cuttingly sharp he couldn't

help but laugh. He tapped his forehead with mock seriousness. "I'm a very astute thinker."

She rolled her eyes playfully and smiled at him. It was nice to see her smiling. She'd been so tense since Enzo's episode. Clearly worried about the boy. So was Marco. He'd always led a pretty adventurous life. Quite a few moments out at sea on his boat had turned harrowing and challenging when an unexpected storm hit midsail.

But he could honestly say Enzo's episode had made him more scared than he'd ever felt.

Enzo twisted in his lap again and kneed him in the groin.

"I told you he wasn't easy in cramped spaces," Brianna said, in response to his grunt. She rummaged in her large bag. "Here, try this." She pulled out a picture book.

Marco opened the book and Enzo seemed mollified for the moment.

Marco glanced at the laptop bag underneath the seat in front of him. "So much for getting some work done on this flight."

"Not unless he falls asleep."

"I'll pray for it."

She shifted in her seat to look at him. "It's quite an adjustment for you, isn't it?" she asked.

"What is?"

"You're always so structured, so in control of your life and your work. Then Enzo and I come along and disrupt it all."

He turned to her. "Is that what you think?"

"Isn't that why you were away from the house so often while we were living there?"

"My work has always taken me away for extended periods. Did you honestly think I was trying to get away from my son?"

She shrugged. "Not necessarily your son. But maybe you wanted to get away from the chaos a child can inflict. Especially one as high energy as Enzo."

"Brianna, I can in all honesty tell you that I never used business as a way to get a reprieve from my child."

"Then perhaps it was a reprieve from the wife you ended up unintentionally saddled with." Brianna bit her lip as soon as the words left her mouth. "I'm sorry, I shouldn't have said that."

He wasn't sure how to respond. She looked away out the window. Marco had to acknowledge the truth in her words. He had thrown himself full force into his work after his marriage. Things had been awkward when she'd first moved in. Neither of them had seemed to know what to say to the other.

Adding to the new dynamic was the reaction of those around them. The whole household, the whole town had seemed infatuated with the newest Dirici. Brianna had found herself the instant subject of unending attention. No doubt some of the buzz had been his own fault. Marco's reputation as a swinging bachelor had taken quite a hit when he'd suddenly gotten married. Everyone who knew him wanted to learn more about the woman who had finally "snared" Marco Dirici.

Judging from her expression right now and her words, his absence had bothered her more than he'd noticed.

"The business was in a major growth spurt," he told her. "It still is. I couldn't ignore that."

"Is that the only reason you had to be away so often? Or for so long?"

"What else?"

"I don't know. Maybe when you were at work you could pretend none of it had ever happened."

There was clear hurt in her voice. How could he have missed it? Things were just so hectic during the months after Brianna had first moved to Italy. She'd been on bed rest for a considerable amount of time. He'd wanted to make sure she got all the rest she needed. And he'd been in the middle of a major expansion with Dirici enterprises.

"I was simply trying to catch up, *cara*."

"Catch up?"

How to explain? Brianna's pregnancy had been a variable he hadn't foreseen. Hadn't planned for. It had thrown his whole life plan out of the proverbial window. He rubbed his forehead. "There were things I wanted to have in place before starting a family of my own."

"What kinds of things?"

"For one, I wanted Dirici Foods to have reached a certain standing on the global stage. I've always known I wanted to expand into North America. The more growth, the more financial security."

"What else?"

What was the point of getting into all this? Her expression told him she really needed an answer. "I guess I always thought I'd be…older when I started a family."

"More mature?"

He shrugged. "I suppose."

She sighed. "Yeah, me too."

Marco reached over to tousle his son's hair. Enzo gave him an adorable smile then started sucking his thumb.

"So you were racing against time to cover the distance you'd lost?" Brianna said. "That's why you were gone so often and for so long."

He supposed that was an interesting way to put it. Accurate, as well.

"It wasn't like you'd been left alone," he argued, though it sounded weak even to his own ears. "Nonna practically doted on you since the day you arrived. Not to mention, we have a full staff at the mansion who are practically family."

A cloud of emotion flooded her eyes. "None of that is the same as having one's husband around."

The words shocked him. He knew she spoke the truth. She was right about him grappling with his new reality when they'd arrived. He'd always had full control of his life and emotions. Then suddenly he found himself a married man with a small child. A wife he could barely contain himself around. It was easier just to stay away and focus on what he was good at. Being a businessman.

She shrugged. "I just finally decided it was fair to move on with my life since you were so consumed with your own," Brianna said, looking out the window.

Marco took a moment to let that sink in. For the past six months he'd come to all sorts of conclusions about why his wife may have left. All his theories had revolved around her. Not once had he considered how his own actions may have led to her decision. Until now.

He had not, by any means, been purposely avoiding her. Had he?

She tightened her seat belt and turned in her seat, reclining back as she did so. "Read the book to Enzo, Marco."

CHAPTER SEVEN

IT WAS LIKE stepping back in time. After a long, exhausting flight during which Enzo grew more and more restless, Brianna found herself finally stepping into the large Mediterranean-style mansion that had been the Dirici home for close to a century. Up until six months ago, it had been her home as well. It certainly didn't feel that way now. Actually, she thought, as she followed Marco through the front door, it had never really felt like home for her. Despite all her attempts to fit in here, and despite all the kindness Marco's staff and grandmother had shown her, she'd always felt out of place. Everything from not being fluent in Italian to the unfamiliarity of the countryside served as a barrier to feeling as if she belonged.

Enzo was clearly a different story.

His baby squeals of joy echoed through the foyer as they entered the house. How could a toddler so small even know? But he seemed completely familiar as he looked over the pillars at the base of the stairs, the high ceilings and the shiny marble tiles on the floor.

A horde of people descended on them at once. The Diricis' housekeeper, doormen, even the cook who'd always treated Brianna like an imposter looking to take over the kitchen.

"Ms. Brianna, so glad to have you back."

"We've missed you both, Ms. Brianna."

So many words of welcome echoed around her, Brianna wasn't even sure who said what. A strange emotion swelled in her chest and she felt a slight sting in her eyes. Enzo was getting even more attention. And he clearly enjoyed it. In his father's arms, he pumped his legs furiously, laughing and gurgling at everyone.

"Where is he? Where is my precious, precious little boy?"

Nonna rushed toward them with her heavy waddle and trademark neck scarf. Today it was a pretty red one with a paisley pattern. She seemed every bit as matronly as Brianna remembered. It was an act. Marie Dirici was as far from a matron as a bull. She was closer to a force of nature. Made all the more effective by her demure disguise.

Nonna wasted no time in pulling Enzo out of Marco's arms and into hers. For a moment, Enzo seemed to disappear in his great-grandmother's ample bosom. When he reemerged, he appeared a little disoriented. His smile returned even wider when Nonna handed him a chocolate biscotti.

Then she turned her attention to Brianna. "Dearest Brianna, how are you, my child?" Brianna found herself in the same tight bear hug.

The greeting both surprised and warmed her. Brianna had, after all, been the reason Nonna and Enzo had been separated for all these months.

"I'm fine, Nonna. You're looking well." The woman was absolutely beaming.

"I'm more than well. Now that you and Enzo are back."

Nonna turned to Marco and placed a large hand on his cheek. "Thank you for bringing them back home."

Brianna waited for Marco to say something, to state the truth behind their return. Nonna had to know this was just a temporary arrangement.

He simply nodded. "Why don't you hold on to

Enzo while I help Brianna get settled," Marco said, taking Brianna by the elbow and leading her up the stairs. Carlo, the Diricis' valet, followed behind with the rest of her luggage.

Brianna took a deep breath. She would make sure to set things straight with Nonna as soon as she could. Right now, she could use some time to freshen up a bit and be alone. All those hours in such close proximity to Marco had taken their toll on her emotions. Everything could wait while she took a breather and adjusted to the time and climate change.

She also had to adjust to the return to a life she thought she'd abandoned for good. Even if it was only temporary.

Brianna found them on the veranda. Marco, Enzo and Nonna sat on the plush wicker patio furniture with a pitcher of iced coffee. Marco's face was hidden behind a newspaper, his foot resting casually on the chair opposite him.

Nonna had Enzo perched on her knee. They were looking at a photo album. Enzo dropped it and ran to Brianna when he noticed her.

She felt a silly sense of relief, that even with

all the excitement and attention, he still reacted to the sight of his mother.

"Did you get a chance to freshen up, dear?" Nonna asked with a warm smile.

"Yes, thank you."

"Come sit. Shall Violetta bring you some tea? I know how much you enjoy it in the afternoon."

She shook her head. "I'll just run down to the kitchen and get some later."

"The kitchen," Nonna said and smiled. "I'll have you know, Marisa made sure all your cooking tools remained exactly as they were. Wouldn't let anyone touch them. Kept saying you'd want them where you'd left them when you returned."

Brianna forced a weak smile. "That was nice of her."

"We're just glad you're back to use them again."

Brianna gave Marco a sharp look, waiting for him to say something. The newspaper remained where it was.

"I must thank her," she said.

In a gesture she wasn't sure what to make of, Enzo gave her leg a hard squeeze, then ran back to Nonna. He scampered up to her lap, the photo book once more in his hands. He opened it up and pointed to one of the pages.

Nonna laughed indulgently. "I take it that's my hint to get started again."

Brianna watched the two of them as she pulled out a chair at the table and dropped herself into it. Enzo certainly did seem happy. Rarely had she seen him act quite this enthusiastic. Sure, he'd always been an energetic, loud, rambunctious little boy. But the grin between his chubby cheeks right now and the pleasure radiating from his eyes were altogether new.

Something squirmed in the bottom of Brianna's belly. She had taken Enzo away from all this. Was that separation really the true source of his issues today?

Enzo let out a squeal of laughter in response to something his great-grandmother said. It had been a while since Brianna had heard him laugh like that. He pointed to something on the page. "Mama."

Nonna nodded. "That's Mama, yes."

He moved his pudgy finger an inch. "Papa."

"Yes, that's right," Nonna answered.

Enzo looked up at Brianna. Then he switched

his gaze to his father. "Wuv Mama. Wuv Papa."
He started to clap.

Brianna's heart gave a thud. Marco finally lowered the newspaper. What in the world was she to do now?

Marco watched the myriad of emotions that drifted over Brianna's face. He watched her features tighten, the way she sucked in her lower lip.

She looked so wistful, so sad. So alone. Was that how she'd felt before she left six months ago?

...wasn't the same as having one's husband around.

He stood and extended a hand to her. "Here. Let's go."

"Where are we going?"

"I could use a walk. There's been several additions to the vineyards. I'll show them to you."

Brianna stared at him a moment, then finally stood without taking his hand. Marco took her gently by the elbow and led her off the veranda.

"Be right back, Nonna," he said over his shoulder.

"Those two are getting along splendidly, aren't they?" Brianna asked after they'd walked a few steps.

"Nonna's always enjoyed his company."

"He's always so well-behaved around her."

"Unlike with all his nannies?"

"All except for—" Brianna stopped.

Marco sighed. "You were going to say Curtis, weren't you?"

She gave him a sideways look and nodded.

"Don't worry," Marco replied. "I'm not going to go rabid at the sound of his name."

"Back in the States, you said he might be trying to manipulate me. What does that mean, exactly?"

"Is it so hard to understand? You're a mature woman, fairly established. He must know you have financial resources. I'd say it was fairly obvious."

"In other words, he may be a gold digger?"

"He wouldn't be the first one I've encountered in my lifetime. I was going to allow you to hire Curtis back, remember?"

"Only after I managed to convince you Curtis would never take money he hadn't earned."

"Yes, well he'd be the rare exception."

She huffed out a small laugh. "Are you saying some of the ladies you've dated were only after you for your money? I find it hard to believe. Handsome and charming as you are."

A childish surge of male pride went through him at her words. Immature as it may be, he liked it that she saw him that way. "I wasn't referring to my past dalliances."

Her eyes grew wide as fire ignited in the green depths. "Then who? You can't mean—"

"Of course not, *cara*. I've never entertained that notion."

"Nor should you." She hesitated before continuing. "Do you mean your mother?"

Marco looked off into the horizon. Thick fluffy clouds glided slowly across the sky. "Even as a child I could see my mother was only in it for the money. The lifestyle."

"She was?"

He nodded. "It was no coincidence that her frequent absences started right around the time the company started floundering." His chest tightened with anger. "The funny thing is, she's partly the reason for the company's financial woes at the time."

"How so?"

"My father was so distracted by his new bride,

he sorely neglected his duties as head of Dirici Foods. Not to mention all the money he spent on her. It was a vicious cycle. The more he tried to appease her, the worse things got. Till one day she left for good."

Brianna started to reach for him. For one insane moment, he waited for her touch, yearned for it. To feel her soft skin against his. She pulled back and brought her fingers to her lips instead. "I'm sorry. For what you had to deal with. As a child."

He shrugged. "Don't feel sorry for me. I had Nonna. My dad was the one who never really recovered. Continued to pine for her. Like a lovesick fool. For years." He grunted in disgust.

"So Nonna came to care for you."

Marco leaned forward on the gate and rested his chin on his forearms. "There was no one else to do it. My father was barely functioning at that point."

"And he withdrew from his only child." She blew out a breath. "You never told me if she ever came back to even visit."

"At first she did. And for those brief moments it felt as if the world was right once more. For me, anyway. She was refreshed, joyous almost. She'd actually get down in the dirt and play with her child. As if she'd found her true nature again."

"That must have been so confusing for you as a small child."

"In any case, what happened with my mother has nothing to do with what's going on with Enzo."

"Maybe. Maybe not."

Whatever she meant by that, he was in no mood to delve into it. What use was it to wallow in the past? It was all water under the bridge. Muddy, filthy water.

"At least you had Nonna," Brianna said, with a wistful hitch in her tone.

Thank the heavens. "And Nonno, for a good while." A pressing thought suddenly occurred to him. What a selfish dolt he could be. Brianna was an orphan, abandoned at birth. She'd never even known her biological mother and father. So while he'd had loving grandparents to bear the load and lessen his pain of abandonment, Brianna had had no one that he knew of.

"It couldn't have been easy for you either, *cara*. Growing up the way you did."

She looked away. "The worst part was just moving from household to household as a foster kid. None of those places had a stable enough environment to last long. And I was hoisted away once again. A different town, a different school. It was impossible to make friends."

Marco plucked a grape and pretended to study it. He waited; she would continue if she wanted. But he was beginning to understand Brianna's fierce desire for independence, to provide stability and grounding for herself and her child.

"There was one home that actually felt safe. Loving. My foster mom was pretty young at heart, so to speak. It was like living with a loving older sister." After a while, she took a deep breath. "She was a former dancer."

"You mean she was in the ballet?"

She laughed. "No, her form of dancing was a bit more, um, exotic than the ballet."

Marco's brows lifted to his hairline. "You're kidding?"

Brianna had to laugh. "No. She'd cleaned up her act and had procured more traditional employment by the time she applied to foster children. But she still had connections to that world.

Enough so that she still danced occasionally to make ends meet. Once that tidbit was discovered we were removed."

"I see." Marco still looked shocked at what she was revealing.

"Foolish really, the most loving home they'd put me in but they deemed it inappropriate." Brianna said the last word as she gestured with hand quotes. She was smiling, but Marco could see the hurt underlying her casual words. "Ironically, it was really the only place I felt like I fit in. Like I belonged."

That included this home too, Marco had no doubt. Brianna had never felt like she fitted in here with him at the Dirici estate. He had to acknowledge that. And the pain it must have caused her.

She reached for a grape and threw it in the air, catching it in her mouth. The innocent gesture gave him a glimpse of the child she must have been. A terribly lonely and solitary one apparently. Yet that unfortunate history had done nothing to diminish her spirit.

Silly really, to be finding out so much about his wife this late in the game. He looked at her carefully; her brow was creased, a troubled frown

framed her lips. She was beautiful. An enchanting princess. She brushed past him further into
the fields. He wanted to stop her, to pull her toward him, to kiss that frown away until she was
moaning beneath him, until she forgot everything
but Marco Dirici. The buzz of his phone with an
incoming text snapped him out of the senseless
thought.

"Looks like Nonna might be our most preferred
parenting guide," Marco said dryly, ignoring the
message on his phone. "Perhaps we should for-
mulate our own parenting scheme then. Not pro-
ceed by example."

"I've been thinking along those lines myself."

"Yeah?"

Brianna wiped her brow with the back of her
hand. The afternoon had grown fairly warm for
this time of year. "Well, maybe we should take
Enzo to see someone. You know, a professional."

"You want to take him to a, how do you Americans say it, a shrink?"

"I think we should consider it."

"I fail to see what good that would do."

"It would help to chart any progress."

Suddenly Marco understood. "And it might

let you know when it's safe to take him back to New York."

She was silent. For several moments, neither of them spoke. Finally, she looked away, out into the distance. "I can't stay here forever, Marco. There are things back in New York waiting for me."

Marco remained where he was though he wanted to go grab hold of her and shake her, demand to know exactly why. She hadn't been in his house a full day yet and she was already figuring out how and when to leave. What was he supposed to do? Beg her to stay with him?

Out of the question. There was no point in prolonging the inevitable.

"It's hot and my appointment is approaching," he said. Even as he made the statement, his phone went off with a series of texts and buzzing sounds. Someone was desperately trying to get a hold of him from the corporate office. He swore as the signal dropped. Reception out here was spotty at best. "We should probably head back," he said, begrudging the intrusion.

A cloud of disappointment washed over Brianna's features. "I'd like to stay awhile longer, if you don't mind."

He didn't feel right leaving her. But the calls and texts were coming in fast and furious now. And he hated to take her away from the serenity of the vineyard. Shame he couldn't stay longer himself.

He would have to make a point of it to come out here more often. With Brianna.

"I trust you haven't been gone so long that you can't find your way back."

She nodded. "I won't be long behind you."

An insane urge to ignore the calls tempted him. But in the end discipline won out. After all, she'd said he was free to go. One of them should be able to enjoy the day out here. And the walk back alone would give him some time to process everything he'd just learned. Not only about his wife, but about himself.

He gave Brianna a small nod and turned to go.

CHAPTER EIGHT

BRIANNA BLEW A tuft of hair off her face as she watched Marco walk away. As much as she would have preferred he stayed, she didn't want to push. Some of what he'd said on the plane about being established financially fell into place now. She'd had no idea just how insecure he was about finances. Just went to show, sometimes even a vast amount of money wasn't enough.

He'd revealed quite a bit, in fact. A lot of it rather surprising.

They'd been so guarded with each other all this time. So distant. But now their little boy's well-being was at stake. They had to make peace with each other, if not as man and wife then as co-parents. Understanding one another better would make significant strides toward that end.

She walked further into the vineyard. It was so peaceful out here, so serene. She had to enjoy it awhile longer. Enzo was in fine hands with

Nonna. It was a beautiful afternoon and Brianna had nothing to do, really. She would just stay out here, walk along the property, take in all the beauty of this enchanting land.

A solitary stroll would help clear her mind. That was the most she and Marco had ever confided in each other. It was a small start, but it was something.

Marco had seemed genuinely disappointed at having to leave her.

His expression before he left reminded her of the night of Enzo's nightmare. How vulnerable Marco had looked when he'd held and rocked Enzo as he comforted him.

That was dangerous territory. Seeing Marco as vulnerable or weak in any way would be a mistake on her part.

So she wouldn't think about how boyish his eyes had appeared beyond the hardened masculinity of his face as he spoke of his childhood. And she absolutely refused to think about the way he'd made her feel in the field earlier, nor the scent of him wafting up to her, or the hardness of his thigh when it had rubbed up against her leg mistakenly during the plane ride.

She squeezed her eyes shut. As a matter of fact, she wouldn't think about anything at all. She'd just enjoy her surroundings. This area of the property was very new. She'd just stay here and see how Marco had expanded the varieties of grapes, what new vintages he was experimenting with. In a couple of years, she was certain he would be a prime supplier of Italian wines to fine restaurants all over the world. He was already one of the leading suppliers of fine Italian olive oils and specialty vinegars. And Dirici Foods was also a top company serving as middleman in acquiring and distributing fine cheeses and premade desserts. To think he'd done it all as practically an orphan, with a mother who'd left and a father too broken to care. The new knowledge added another dimension to the man she'd married but hadn't really ever known.

Brianna had no doubt he would be just as successful when the wine was ready. He would start small, providing a few bottles to local restaurants. And in no time, he'd grow that aspect of the business too. He was smart, dedicated—

She huffed out a breath.

So much for taking him off her mind. She had

to figure out a way to wipe Marco out of her brain. She'd rather focus on the beautiful afternoon air, the wonderful smell of the grapes, the acres and acres of lush green grass that stretched out far into her line of vision.

Too far.

She paused and looked around. And come to think of it, the smell of the grapes was no longer nearly as pungent. She looked up to see she wasn't even in the vineyard anymore.

Brianna turned. The house was no longer visible. The time had passed quickly. She had to turn around or she'd never have enough time to get cleaned up before dinner. In this part of the world, the evening meal was a nightly event one didn't simply just show up for. Particularly not after strolling through dusty fields and working up a sweat.

She started walking toward the road. Within no time, the fashionable sandals on her feet felt like torture devices. Definitely not shoes meant for long trails through the Italian countryside. She was so busy cursing her lack of a decent sense of direction that it took a while to notice the distant whir of a car engine. Behind her. She turned around as the car drew alongside her, breathing a sigh of relief when she recognized the person in the driver's seat.

Leonardo Soldaro. Marco's business associate and childhood friend. She'd met Leo several times. He was funny and charming, one of the people who had made her feel at ease when she'd first married Marco and moved out here.

Brianna couldn't help the grin that spread across her face. The car stopped a few feet in front of her and Leo got out.

"Brianna. Is that you?" He walked toward her, the car still running.

"No other."

"You're back then." He was a foot from her now and leaned in to give her a small peck on both cheeks.

"Just a few hours ago."

"What in the world are you doing out here?"

She laughed. "Quite foolishly, I wandered too far after Marco and I parted ways back at the vineyards."

Leo's smile deepened. "I can't believe that fool of a man lets you out of his sight at all."

"Still as charming as ever, I see."

"Yes, perhaps you could persuade others, particularly those of your fine gender, of the extents of my charm."

"I certainly will. Who would you like me to start with?" she asked, just to humor him. Leo had a reputation throughout this whole side of Italy when it came to women. It rivaled only Marco's. That thought ebbed the tide of her pleasure so she pushed it aside.

"Well, come then." He guided her to the car. "I was actually headed to see that thickheaded associate of mine. He picked a most inopportune time to chase you back to the States, you know. Several things need immediate attention."

Brianna didn't bother to argue that point. The notion that Marco would jeopardize even the smallest business matter for her sake was quite laughable. His son, however, was another matter. Enzo was the real reason Marco had flown to New York. Not her.

She crawled into the stylish convertible and sucked in her breath as air fanned her face when Leo started to drive. It was too pleasant in the cool, comfortable car to utter more than a few words. Leo asked about her son but for the most part they rode in silence. She watched the beautiful scenery whiz by and thanked the heavens that Leo had come upon her when he did.

"Where have you been? I've been worried out—" Marco's words died on his lips as Brianna stepped into the foyer followed by Leo right on her heels.

"I wasn't gone that long, Marco."

She was right, it hadn't been that long. And clearly she was safe and sound. So why was his blood pounding in his veins? He had to admit it was guilt. He'd felt guilty for leaving her, even though she'd said it was all right.

The matter he'd been summoned about wasn't even anything that pressing. He'd regretted it immediately once he'd gotten back to his study. And like the bastard that he was, he was oh, so ready to take it out on her. To make matters worse, another man had come to her assistance when he had left her alone.

Quite the husband, he was. How many instances had there been in the time Brianna had lived here that he'd been as equally inconsiderate? Downright cadlike?

He pinched the bridge of his nose. "You're

right. I was simply concerned as I thought you'd be fairly close behind me."

Leo wasn't even hiding his smirk at Marco's agitated state. "I found Brianna wandering by the main road. I gave her a lift on my way over here."

"How gallant of you," Marco stated, his voice dripping with such sarcasm that it earned a gasp from Brianna. Leo simply barked out a laugh.

"Well, thanks again for the ride." Brianna headed toward the stairs, clearly having had enough of the both of them. "I'm going to go get cleaned up."

Marco turned toward his study and motioned for Leo to follow. They had several items to discuss now that Marco had returned and he had to get his mind in gear.

"It's really too bad that we have so much business to go over this afternoon." Leo made the mundane announcement as he strode into the study and sat in the chair opposite Marco's desk.

"And why is that?" Marco hoped Leo's usual penchant for small talk could somehow be cut short this day. He was in no mood for it.

"Because you look like you could use a drink."

"Thanks for that observation," Marco said dryly.

Leo's gaze sharpened. "Tell me what's going on."

"I can give you the New York updates later. I thought you were here to tell me about some critical issues. I'm guessing the pasta project has hit a snag." Marco pulled a file from the corner of his desk and opened it, then punched in the appropriate keys on his laptop to call up the information.

He looked up to see Leo staring at him intently, his fingers steepled in front of his face.

"I mean with you and Brianna," Leo said.

Marco's first urge was to tell him to mind his own business. Especially where Brianna was concerned. He still didn't like the way they'd looked when they'd walked in together. Nor the way Leo had come across Brianna so conveniently.

"She's back for Enzo's sake," Marco said. "Nothing more. Once we figure out the best way to help him adjust to our separation, she will return to New York."

"I see," was all Leo said.

Marco lifted an eyebrow. Leo's comment definitely held a certain tone to it. "Something you'd like to say?" he asked, knowing he would regret the question.

He was right. "I can't believe you'd be fool enough to let that woman go. Again."

Marco sighed. As if Nonna wasn't bad enough. He really didn't feel like taking this from Leo as well.

"Whatever the issue is, I'm sure it's your doing," Leo boldly added as only a lifelong best friend could. Even still, his remark bordered rather close to uncalled for.

Marco didn't rise to the bait, he was simply too weary. "We have a few issues we need to address, if you must know."

"Such as?"

"Such as we don't really seem to know each other that well."

Leo nodded with satisfaction. "See, I knew it. It is all your doing. You're way too closed off, too guarded. Always have been."

"How is this any of your concern?" Marco demanded to know, barely acknowledging that the other man's comment had hit too close.

Leo shrugged. "It's not. I just try to steer you in the right direction. But you often refuse to listen."

He really was too much. "You've had your say, Leo. Now we really should get to work."

Leo hesitated before nodding slowly. The next few hours passed at a hectic pace. Leo was right. Several details needed Marco's immediate attention. He had to schedule an on-site visit to the Rome distribution center as soon as possible. The new project leader had been remiss to say the least. Marco realized he should have given Leo more authority before he'd left. By the time Violetta knocked on the door to announce supper, he was surprised just how much time had passed.

"You will join us?" he asked Leo, knowing Nonna would have his hide if he didn't.

"No. I should head back. I have a dinner meeting."

Marco stood and dropped his pen. "Knowing you, I doubt it involves much of a meeting. Or dinner for that matter."

Leo flashed him a grin. "It wasn't so long ago that you had those same 'meetings', my friend." Leo stood too. "Speaking of which, I should like to say goodbye to that beautiful wife of yours before I leave."

Marco knew Leo well enough to realize the

mischievous set of his mouth, and to take notice of the merriment dancing around the other man's eyes. But try as he might, he just couldn't resist the need to respond to his goad.

"I think you've spent enough time with my beautiful wife today. You are quite fortunate we're not outside *discussing* that issue right now."

Leo barked out a laugh. "For Enzo's sake, you said. Right."

Before Marco had a chance to comment on that, Brianna knocked and stepped into the room. "Nonna wants to make sure you invite Leo to eat with us." She was glaring at Marco, as if she had no desire to speak to him at all. But when she turned to Leo, her face was all smiles. Marco had a sudden urge to punch Leo in the nose.

"I'm afraid I can't stay, love," Leo said as he walked toward her. He kissed her cheek. "I shall see myself out."

"You do that," Marco said.

Leo laughed and shut the door behind him.

Brianna made her way downstairs and into the dining room to join the others. To her surprise, Marco was the only other person at the table.

"Where's Nonna?" she asked, pulling out a chair and sitting down across from him.

"Apparently, she's not feeling very well and decided to skip dinner."

Alarm raced through her chest. Nonna wasn't exactly a young woman. "I hope it's nothing serious."

Marco gave a nonchalant shrug. "Probably her arthritis. It always acts up before rainstorms."

As if responding to his words, a big flash of lightning lit up the sky in the window behind him.

Marco didn't seem all that concerned about Nonna's health. She decided to take his cue. But then a twinge of apprehension started to take hold for an entirely different reason. The scene she and Marco found themselves was almost intimate. Just the two of them, right before a storm, the lights of the room dimmed low. She cleared her throat and tried to reach for a topic that might make for small talk. She came up blank for an immeasurable amount of time.

Marco, for his part, didn't make any attempt at conversation.

"The grapes seemed to have fared well," she

ventured, grabbing a crusty focaccia from the bread bowl. "Looks like a good harvest."

He nodded. "If the weather holds all season, we should do very well."

A flicker of pride fluttered through her chest. Her husband was skilled at so many things. "You must be so proud," she began. "A successful winery would add yet another dimension to Dirici Foods. All thanks to you."

"I've been thinking about it for years, getting into the wine business." Brianna couldn't help but notice that he said it with an odd laugh.

She looked at him in question. "Why do you find that laughable?"

"You wouldn't understand."

Oh, no, not this again. She thought they'd made some strides in the vineyards earlier. Was he really going to backtrack yet again?

Marco must have sensed the direction of her thoughts. He put down his knife and fork to level her with an unflinching gaze. "It's just that I'd planned on having so much in place for Dirici Foods before a certain…age, shall we say."

He may have said "age" but she knew what he

really meant. Perhaps she shouldn't have pushed after all. "You mean before you started a family."

Marco didn't blink. "I don't regret our son, Brianna. You must not ever think that."

Of course she didn't think so. But the fact had to be acknowledged that Enzo was the result of an unplanned pregnancy. Someone like Marco who planned everything out with meticulous detail, who'd had to endure the abandonment of both parents, would have certainly hoped to have a bit more control over starting a family, raising a child.

In that regard they weren't terribly different, were they?

She swallowed down the lump of emotion that had suddenly formed at the base of her throat. "I know that, Marco. I really do. I think we both have to just admit that each of us was unprepared in a different way. That doesn't make us less loving or enamored with our child."

His shoulders seemed to drop with relief. Somehow, she'd managed to say the right thing. But it was her heartfelt truth.

He waited a beat before picking up his utensils once more. "In fact, I'm thinking about taking

Enzo down to see the vines. I think he'll enjoy seeing the rows and rows of hanging fruit."

"I'm sure he'll love it, now that he's old enough to appreciate it a bit. Though he's much too young to truly fathom just how fortunate he is to have all that land at his disposal."

Marco paused in the act of piercing some gnocchi with his fork. "You were placed in mostly inner-city homes, weren't you?"

She nodded. "Not a lot of land to run around or play. You were lucky to have it as a child."

Marco swallowed. "Yes, well. I didn't always feel so lucky."

He wouldn't have. Not as his family was falling apart around him. It was yet another lesson in looks being deceiving. A heavy silence settled between them, suddenly turning the moment awkward. Brianna cleared her throat.

"You might want to be careful while you're out there with him," she said teasingly, to lighten the mood.

He looked up at her with question. "Why's that?"

She finished a bite of bread before answering him. "To a toddler, all those grapes are simply going to look like numerous little balls that he can launch and throw. I'm guessing you'll both be quite sticky afterward." That image prompted a giggle to erupt from her throat.

"You would find that funny, would you?" Marco asked with mock offense.

"Very."

"If that's the case, there's really only one thing I'd be curious about," he said.

"What would that be?"

"How good is his throwing arm?"

Brianna smiled at the silly question. "Quite capable actually. He likes to throw slightly bigger objects, like his sippy cups usually. But tiny orbs that explode on impact would provide him immense entertainment, I'm sure."

"Good to know. As an Italian, I would have preferred a football—sorry, soccer—playing son but baseball's a respectable sport for you Americans."

That comment led to a particularly heated discussion about the merits of one sport over the other. By the time they finished eating and started clearing the dishes, Brianna was relieved to find that the awkwardness of earlier had completely dissipated.

In fact, it had been a surprisingly enjoyable

dinner overall. She was discovering more about Marco since returning to Italy than she had the entire time she'd lived with him.

He was finally opening up to her. She could only hope it would last. She had to admit, after all this time, it was nice finally getting to know her husband. Even if it was much too late to save their marriage.

Bright sunshine flooded into the room from the window across the bed. It didn't seem right, Brianna thought, slowly coming awake. Not after listening to the rain and thunder for most of the night.

Someone had brought in a pot of coffee sometime during the early morning hours. She stood and poured herself a cup, drinking it quickly. It had gone completely cold but the caffeine nevertheless did its job.

Scenes from the previous day ran through her mind like a movie. Marco's look as he'd talked about his mother leaving when he was just a small child.

She remembered the way he had opened up to her earlier in the day, and the lighthearted banter during dinner.

The way she'd bared a bit of her soul so that he may offer a glimpse of his. Brianna sighed and poured herself another cup, walking to the bathroom as she drank. A long, hot shower would feel like heaven. She felt like she'd lived about a year in the last few days alone.

After that, she wanted to go find Enzo. She couldn't even remember the last time he'd woken up to anyone else besides his mama.

When she made it downstairs she found Nonna on the front veranda sipping tea and nibbling on her usual light breakfast of toast and fruit with a full pot of espresso. Brianna felt a sense of relief that she was feeling better. When she saw her, Nonna welcomed her with a large smile.

"Brianna, darling. Please do join me."

"I'd love to. Where's Enzo?"

"Marco took him out about half an hour ago, dear. They're walking to the pond. He said he wanted to show Enzo how full it gets after a storm such as the one last night."

"Oh," Brianna said with disappointment, realizing she'd dearly missed her son.

Brianna pulled out a chair and sat. Violetta immediately appeared with a full cup of coffee and a basket of the baked goods Brianna enjoyed so much. The comfort and luxury of the Dirici estate was not something she'd gotten used to even while living here.

"We missed you at dinner yesterday," Brianna said, peering at her over her cup. "Are you all right?"

The older woman gave a dismissive wave of her hand. "It was nothing. Just feeling a little weary in these old bones. I'm good as rain."

"Glad to hear it, Nonna. We can't have you not feeling well."

"And I'm glad we have a chance to speak, dear. It's been ages since I've been able to really talk to you." She set her cup down. "How have you been? Truly?"

Brianna shrugged. Despite not having known her all that long, Nonna was as dear to her as anyone. More of a maternal figure than any other lady in her life, Nonna was just one of those people who always made others comfortable. But Brianna's emotions were too close to the surface to risk a heart-to-heart chat right now.

"We've been adjusting," she answered.

"You both seem terribly worried about Enzo. He seems like a perfect little boy to me."

Brianna sighed. "For the most part he is, Nonna. He just has some…issues. Disciplinary and otherwise."

"You mean about his nannies."

Brianna nodded. "Among other things. He's only a baby really. But once he decides he doesn't like someone, he's pretty much made up his mind. It's becoming embarrassing how many sitters I've had to employ."

"Tell me, then. In the beginning, does he give these nannies a chance?"

Brianna squinted in the early morning sun. "I suppose."

"Ah," was all Nonna said.

Brianna waited for her to continue. For several moments, it didn't appear as if she would. Finally, Nonna spoke.

"Don't you understand then, dear?" she asked.

Brianna shook her head. Understand what?

"Enzo isn't overly rambunctious. He just isn't terribly forgiving after a transgression." She patted Brianna's hand. "Perhaps at some point these nannies uttered a harsh reprimand, or ignored a plea, or any number of things that a small boy wouldn't understand. It's a genetic trait, I dare say."

"You're saying it might be enough to color his impression of that person." Brianna put her pastry down and leaned back into her chair. "It's a trait he gets from Marco, isn't it?"

"I'm afraid so, dear. He also doesn't tolerate transgression very well."

Did Marco see her leaving as such a transgression? And what did that mean for her if he did?

"Well, no matter now," Nonna declared. "All that matters is that you and Enzo are back."

"I only came back because of Enzo." Nonna had to realize this wasn't meant to be a reunion between man and wife.

Nonna smiled slightly. "So you both keep telling me."

Brianna found she didn't have the stomach to try and belabor the point right now. Nor the desire to continue eating. And the third cup of coffee on a relatively empty stomach was starting to make her insides churn. She wiped her lips with her napkin and stood. "Please excuse me, Nonna. I really would like to go find my son."

"I think you should, dear. Of course you remember where the pond is."

"I do," Brianna replied, and started making her way to it.

The air felt crisp around her. Each light breeze brought with it the delicate scent of the ripe wine grapes. Marco's lands were lush and beautiful. And very vast. The vineyard hadn't even been part of the Dirici estate when Marco had inherited it. He'd expanded his lands just as he'd expanded the business. Under Marco's management, Dirici Foods had gone from a small Italy-based company to a major global supplier to fine restaurants everywhere.

He was a complex, multidimensional man. One she admired and respected. But was he one she could live with? It was obvious they cared for each other and of course there was the fierce attraction.

And given what Nonna had just told her, Brianna didn't think she'd have too many opportunities to figure it all out. If things didn't work out between them this time, Marco would close the door behind her and their previous life together without looking back. She'd already figured that, Nonna had just further clarified.

The fact was, a part of her had wished Marco had asked her not to leave six months ago—a truth she was finally allowing herself to acknowledge. But her leaving seemed to have triggered something. It was almost as if they were meeting for the first time, without the pressures of an unexpected whirlwind marriage hindering them as they got to know each other.

Brianna finally approached the small hill overlooking the large pond. As she moved closer, Enzo's bubbly chatter punctuated the air. When she made it to the top, she realized with surprise that both Enzo and his father were actually in the water. She noticed the pile of their clothes on the bank. Enzo was laughing now as he kicked water at his father's heels, Marco wore a huge smile on his face and pretended to be upset at being splashed. Brianna's heart warmed. Enzo was clearly enjoying himself. He was completely naked. And Marco wore nothing but shorts.

And sweet heaven, it took her breath away. Even from a distance, his toned muscular body made her heart pound. He was the golden tan color of beach sand. A shade earned from hard work and equally hard play outdoors.

Unlike the men back in New York who worked for their physiques in the gym, Marco achieved his by helping tend to his lands and by sailing competitively. The results were havoc-wreaking.

He's just a man, like any other man, Brianna told herself. A small voice in her head laughed. Marco would never be like any other man she'd ever known.

Marco pretended to fall in the water and Enzo let out another loud squeal of laughter. She was only a few feet away when they finally noticed her.

"What is the meaning of this?" she demanded with mock outrage.

Marco halted. His gaze traveled from her face down the length of her body. Her pulse quickened.

"Mama!" Enzo cried and ran out of the pond to hug her legs, soaking her in the process.

"Good morning, sweet one. What happened to your clothes, huh?"

Enzo just laughed and jumped back in the pond, landing on his feet with an agility that surprised her. She looked back to Marco.

"An early-morning dip," he said by way of explanation. Water streamed down his chest, high-lighting the hard contours. Brianna had to fight not to lick her dry lips. Marco smiled salaciously as if he could read her mind.

"Isn't the water cold? After the storm and everything?"

Marco shook his head, still knee-deep in the pond. "The storm is what's made the water so re-freshing. It's much deeper now. I thought Enzo would enjoy it."

"He most definitely seems to be."

"You should try it out for yourself." Marco made a move toward her. Brianna stepped back quickly.

"Oh, no. I am *not* going in there."

Enzo clapped. "Mama een. Mama een."

Brianna laughed. "No, Mama's not going in."

"We'll see about that," Marco said and moved toward her again.

This time Brianna jumped back. "Don't you come near me," she said, shaking her finger with warning.

Marco stood where he was and lifted an eye-brow. "Enzo, it appears your mother is the typi-cal prissy city girl who's afraid of water."

He said it with such seriousness, Brianna was almost offended. "Hey," she replied. "Not fair. I'll have you know, I was one of the strongest swimmers in summer camp every year."

"In a nice, clean, chlorinated pool I'm sure," Marco said with a shudder.

Brianna crossed her arms in front of her chest. "No, in a large forest pond that would put this puny one to shame."

Marco shook his head as if to clear his ears. "You mock my pond?"

"I would call it a puddle."

He looked up at the sky with a hilariously wounded expression on his face. "You know you're going to have to pay for that insult."

"Awfully sensitive about the size of your water, aren't you?"

This time he smiled at her *double entendre*. "Brianna, Brianna, Brianna," he said. "We're going to have to teach you a lesson." She wasn't sure what he intended and she moved back another step just in case. But then he picked up Enzo and Brianna breathed a sigh of relief. Until he set him down on the bank. Enzo sat down right on the pile of clothes then wrapped himself in his father's once crisp clean shirt.

"Watch this, son."

Before she could make out what he was up to, Marco bolted toward her. Brianna turned and ran, laughter bubbling up in her chest. She wasn't fast enough. Marco's arms snaked around her waist when she hadn't even gone five feet. She felt herself being lifted off the ground.

Marco turned and carried her back toward the bank. Brianna struggled to get out of his arms, but his grip was so tight and by now she was laughing too hard to protest with any conviction.

She stopped laughing when he stepped in the water. "Marco, don't you dare," she said. "I'm warning you. You will regret it."

Enzo continued to sit on the pile of clothes, intermittently giggling and sucking his thumb.

"What have you got to say about my pond now, hmmm?"

Brianna couldn't resist. "You are referring to your puddle, right?"

"My dear, you are in no position to fling further insults." He lowered her an inch or so. She flung her arms around his neck to brace herself.

His reaction was immediate. Brianna suddenly forgot about the threat of being immersed, she forgot about the playful banter. There was a sudden warmth in Marco's eyes, something else entirely mixed in with the amusement.

It hit her full force, how much she cared for this man. She'd fallen in love with him that first week in New York City and she'd never gone back.

He was perfect. He was flawed. He would do anything for his son. Brianna had never come across a father who cared so much. And he made her feel emotions she wouldn't have thought she was capable of. Her expression must have changed because Marco's playful mood suddenly disappeared. His eyes grew even darker.

"Brianna?" he whispered.

Glancing at Enzo to ensure he still sat safely on the grass, she reached up to touch his face, traced his lips with her fingers. She desperately wanted those lips on hers again. She'd never stopped wanting him. But now she wasn't sure at all that she could fight it. Or that she wanted to.

Marco closed his eyes on a sigh and gently kissed her fingertips. Brianna swallowed a moan. She didn't want to lose him again. Maybe there was a way they could work on their differences. Maybe there was a way they could fight for what they had. She pulled her fingers away, inching her head closer to his. Would he respond?

A squeal of delight from her son had her pulling back on a gasp.

"Mama een!"

Marco's eyes snapped open. He looked over at his child and laughed. Just like that, the moment was gone.

"Sir, I demand that you put me down this instant," Brianna said. Her attempt to sound totally authoritative must not have worked.

"If you insist."

Before Brianna could protest that he'd deliberately misread her words, she hit the water with a resounding splash. Landing on her bottom, it took all her arm strength to keep her head above the water line. It was surprisingly clear and much warmer than she'd been expecting.

She was nevertheless stung.

Enzo squealed in delight. Brianna wiped off her face with the palm of her hand.

"You will pay for that."

Marco's grin only widened. "What are you going to do? Splash me? Get me wet?"

Enzo's giggles reverberated in air from where he sat. Brianna dug her hand into the muddy bottom. She lifted her other hand to Marco. "At least help me up."

Marco hesitated, enjoying her predicament. Then he bent down and took her outstretched hand.

She waited until just the right time. One, two...

The mud caught him square on the chin. Marco appeared shocked, even staggered back a bit. Brianna's laugh tore from the depths of her belly. Marco dove in the water, practically on top of her.

"You fight dirty, don't you, dear wife?"

The literal and figurative slant of his words made her laugh even harder. She no longer cared how wet she was.

"Here, let me wipe that off." She brought her hand up to his face, making sure to grab another handful of mud. She slapped it on his cheek.

Marco had been expecting it. He didn't look the least bit surprised. Enzo was laughing so hard, Brianna turned to make sure he wasn't going to fall over and do a face plant on the grass.

It was a mistake. Marco took the opportunity to strike. In one smooth movement, he shifted onto his bottom and sat, pulling her onto his lap. Gripping her by the shoulders, he gently but firmly ducked her further into the water. Brianna sputtered about. She could no longer tell whether she or Enzo was laughing harder. She glanced over her shoulder at Marco. The thick mud still clinging to his face made her laugh even more.

His hand reached in the water and she just knew what he was going for.

She went completely still and made herself stop laughing. "Wait, wait. Hang on." She rubbed her knee. "I think I hurt my leg."

Marco let go of her so fast and he looked so concerned, she felt somewhat guilty. But she didn't hesitate. She sprinted up and made a dash toward dry land.

Again, she wasn't fast enough. Marco pulled her back down and this time moved on top of her to pin her down. And now her shoulders were completely immersed. She couldn't possibly get any wetter.

"Okay, okay," she muttered. "I give."

"You do, huh?"

"Yes."

"Then tell me this is the most magnificent body of water you have ever laid eyes on. That it parallels the mighty oceans—"

Oh, he was too much. Brianna purposely stuck her head in and came back out spitting a stream of water in Marco's face.

This time when Enzo laughed, he did manage to lose his balance and topple himself off the pile of clothing. Brianna and Marco both bolted to his side. Marco lifted him upright. He appeared unharmed and continued to laugh. But definitely dirty. Beyond dirty.

"Perhaps we should head back and get this little one cleaned up," Marco suggested.

"I think you and I could use a hot shower, too."

Heat danced in his eyes. She hadn't meant it that way. But she couldn't help but picture it. Marco feeling her skin as hot water poured over the two of them.

The lightheartedness they'd been enjoying suddenly turned to something else. Brianna stole a glance at Marco. He looked fierce. And determined. The remaining smears of mud on his face made him look like a rugged warrior wearing tribal battle paint. A shudder bolted through her.

She had no doubt his lips would be on hers if the two of them were alone.

She picked up Enzo. "Come on, little guy."

Marco retrieved their clothes and wrapped his shirt tighter around their son. Together, the three of them slowly made their way back to the house. For all the excitement, Enzo appeared spent. And utterly oblivious to the electricity crackling between his parents.

If only she could be equally unaware.

Marco watched Brianna as she cradled Enzo in her arms. She was cuddling him close. Enzo's eyelids started to droop and he looked more than content snuggled up to his mother.

"Looks a little worn out, doesn't he?" he asked.

Brianna smiled and rubbed her cheek against the top of her son's head. She tightened her hold on him. "He doesn't seem to be cold."

Unlike Brianna herself. Marco noticed the goose bumps along her arms. Without thinking, he put his arm around her shoulders.

Brianna looked up at him in surprise but she

didn't say anything. A moment later, he could have sworn she nestled in closer to him. Probably just to keep warm, he told himself. But he felt oddly elated.

It was such a simple thing really. He was walking back to the house with his wife and son. But he'd never felt more content. Despite all his material possessions, he'd never felt wealthier than he did right now. All this time, he'd been busting his butt at the office in order to ensure that he was a good father. Look how that had worked out. Perhaps he should have been doing more of this instead, spending more time just enjoying the family he had.

But at this moment the picture of family harmony was little more than a façade, a fact he had to accept and acknowledge.

He'd had this for real but had somehow blown it. Good fortune was often fleeting.

Neither said anything as they walked slowly back to the house. Enzo's eyelids drooped lower and lower. Finally, the mansion appeared before them.

Nonna opened the door before they'd reached it. "What in the world happened to you three?"

she asked and reached for Enzo who had completely fallen asleep.

"We slipped," Marco replied and gave Brianna a conspiratorial wink. He closed the door behind them. Enzo was so deep in slumber he didn't even awaken when passed over to his grandmother.

"I'll have Violetta brew some espresso," Nonna said. Carlo appeared with three large towels. He handed one to Nonna for Enzo then gave Marco the other. Marco took the third towel from him, perhaps a little abruptly, and wrapped it around Brianna's shoulders.

"You're shaking." Did he dare hope it was due to more than just the cold?

Nonna headed toward the stairs with Enzo in her arms. "I'll try to get him dried off and changed, I hope he doesn't wake up."

"Oh, he won't," Brianna said with a smile at her son. She turned to Marco. "Your boy can sleep through anything."

"Our boy," he corrected her. For some reason he felt the need to reiterate the fact, to remind her of the connection that they would always have, no matter what happened between them in the end.

"You should probably go take a shower. Before you start to smell as bad as the pond."

Brianna gave him a surprised, questioning look. Then a smile pulled at her mouth. She turned toward the bathroom and he couldn't resist giving her a playful pat on the bottom as he followed her upstairs to get cleaned up himself.

Marco made his way up to the suite and made himself wait until his pulse slowed. As much as he wanted to, he wouldn't allow himself to remember those early days when she would have invited him into the shower with her. And he would have wholeheartedly followed. He fisted his hands by his side.

"Marco?"

He leaned closer to her adorably muddy face and gave her the gentlest, merest brush of a kiss.

"Enjoy your shower, *cara*."

CHAPTER NINE

SHE'D BEEN AWAKE for hours before the knock sounded on her door. It was Marco; even the way he knocked had a distinctive quality. Memories of the day before had been rushing through her mind all morning. The way he'd held her. The gentle kiss on her cheek as he'd bade her good-bye.

"Come in."

Marco entered, clasping on his watch as he walked in. He gave her a smile—a lazy, closed smile that didn't quite reach his whole face. A smile that appeared too strained.

His expression told her everything she needed to know. He had withdrawn.

It was all wrong. Things were being left un-said. Again.

He moved over to her and leaning in, gave her a small peck on the cheek. A kiss which held nowhere near the affection of the one yesterday.

"Wanted to check on you. I have a few phone calls to make. Then Leo and I have a meeting."

She nodded silently.

"Is something wrong?" he asked.

Yes, everything. "No, not at all."

Reaching for the robe that lay across the bed, Brianna slipped it on and secured the belt. She made her way over to the vanity and sat down in front of the mirror. With absentminded motions, she ran a brush through her hair. What they'd shared yesterday had been something out of a sweet, romantic movie. But this morning, they were back to acting like strangers.

This was a pattern. Based on past history, such moments of closeness and intimacy were usually followed by days and days of long hours at the office or traveling for work. Other than Marco stopping by during a lunch hour to spend some time with his son, Brianna would barely see him.

A clear withdrawal every time they seemed to get close. He was doing it again. How could she have not seen it coming? Simply because she'd left him six months ago?

"Are you certain there's nothing the matter?" he asked.

She looked up at him in the mirror. Well, she certainly wasn't going to sit around moping.

"Actually, I was going to ask you if Cook could use a day off or two. There are some new recipes I wanted to experiment with. But I don't want to take over her kitchen."

"I'm sure she'll be cooperative. You may even be able to get her to help you."

Brianna shook her head. "No help. I need to work on these all by myself."

"And why is that?"

"Because they'll be my audition dishes. It was a fluke that Chef Angelo Ziyad offered me a job last week."

Marco lifted an eyebrow just as Brianna realized what she'd let slip.

"You were offered a job before we left?"

She nodded.

"That quickly?"

She shrugged. "I told you, it was more of a fluke."

"Chef Ziyad, you said. Sounds familiar."

"He's one of the best."

Marco contemplated her for a moment.

"That's quite impressive. I mean, in the sense

that you'd just gotten started before you had to take an extended break. Then not long after your return to the business, a master chef is already aware of your talents."

He sounded genuinely impressed. Why did that send a giddy pleasure through her heart?

"So what happened? How did you leave it with Chef Ziyad?" he asked.

She shrugged. "I wasn't able to get hold of his assistant. And then it turned out we had to rush here to Italy."

"Why didn't you tell me?"

"There was no point."

"I see," Marco said. He looked up at the ceiling and sighed deeply. "It sounds like quite an opportunity."

Brianna looked down at her toes. "There will be other ones," she stated, not entirely sure who she was trying to convince. "My son comes first."

He shocked her by kissing her full on the lips.

"What was that for?"

"For being such a caring mother." Marco rubbed the back of his hand down her cheek. "I'm ashamed to admit I didn't give your career nearly enough consideration after Enzo was born."

She shook her head. "I don't blame you for that, Marco. I was only focused on one thing right after I gave birth. I was just so grateful that Enzo was born healthy and at full term after all the pregnancy complications. I wanted to concentrate on nothing but being the mother of a newborn."

He nodded. "I know, *cara*. It's why I hired the nannies. To give you a break now and then."

He didn't really understand. She could have never left her baby in the care of strangers for any extended length of time back then. Not when she herself had been abandoned at birth. And with Marco being gone all the time, most of the parenting had fallen to her.

"I wanted to be the one nurturing him when he was born," she countered. "But now that he's a bit older…" She let the sentence drag off.

"What is it?"

Brianna considered telling him what was foremost on her mind. After all, this was the perfect time given the conversation they were surprisingly having. She'd gotten an idea during the early hours of the morning when she couldn't sleep. This had to be some kind of serendipity.

"There's something else I wanted to discuss with you."

He gave her a quizzical look in the mirror. "What would that be?"

"Nonna mentioned Dirici Foods is ready to launch a new line of herb-infused oils, some rather savory combinations."

"We are. And?"

Brianna decided to just blurt it out. What did she have to lose at this point? She had to keep busy while here. And this idea would give her one more thing to do. In the past, she'd nearly been driven insane with Marco constantly gone and Enzo napping a lot of the time.

"I'd like to work on some recipes incorporating the new products." She continued before she could change her mind. "Maybe you could even print them on labels as a marketing strategy."

Marco's eyebrows lifted. High. Brianna held her breath. He hated the idea. Now he had to try and come up with a way to turn her down.

Instead, he surprised her yet again. "*Cara*, that's fantastic."

She blinked. "It is?"

He leaned over and kissed her soundly on the cheek. "Absolutely. It's actually better than anything that's come out of the advertising agency. And it would serve to get you back in the kitchen."

Brianna resisted the urge to pump her fist in the air like an excited teen.

"When can you get started?"

Brianna sucked in some air, nearly dizzy with all the possibilities. This would give her an opportunity to do what she loved most—creating and perfecting recipes in the kitchen.

"This very moment. That is, if Cook will allow it."

"I'll speak to her before starting my calls."

For some reason or another, perhaps unfairly, she'd fully expected him to turn down her offer. That he'd accepted with such enthusiasm pleased her beyond any level she would have thought. "Marco. Thank you," she said simply.

"You can thank me by starting with the rosemary blend. That would make the perfect start for a new marketing initiative."

She would. Brianna could think of numerous

ideas right off the cuff for ways to use rosemary olive oil.

But what exactly did this mean for the two of them?

Of that, she had no idea whatsoever.

Marco stared into Leo's face and tried to focus on what the other man was saying. Something about a supply chain glitch that had been repaired easily enough but that Marco should be aware of. But his thoughts kept drifting back to Brianna and the developments of this morning.

He'd clearly underestimated Brianna's talent and possibilities as a chef. She'd thrown herself wholeheartedly into motherhood after having Enzo. Marco had never realized how much of her identity and self she'd sacrificed in the process.

Shame on him for that.

"And then the project leader grew another head," Leo said across the desk.

Marco nodded. "Well, make sure you tell—" *Wait a minute.* He threw his pen down and leaned back in his chair.

Leo sat grinning. "You haven't been listening to a thing I said."

"There's a lot on my mind."

"Are you thinking about the regatta? It's still a while away."

He was referring to the sailing boat race along the Amalfi coast that both men participated in every year. In fact, Marco had almost completely forgotten about it. No wonder, between the demands of Dirici Foods and with all that was happening in his personal life.

"No, that's not it. Though I do look forward to beating you yet again."

"As if," Leo said, then looked at him expectantly. Marco really didn't want to get into all this. No better time than the present though.

"Leo, are you still interested in doing more at Dirici Italy?" Marco hadn't even realized he was ready to ask Leo such a question. But he thought about the days he'd spent in New York, away from Dirici headquarters. The time he'd been able to devote to just being with his son while there. And how gratifying it had been just to spend a few hours with him kicking around in the pond.

He thought of Brianna and all she had put aside without ever even dwelling on it or questioning it.

Leo sat gaping at him. "Of course I am. What did you have in mind?"

A rapid knock sounded on the door just before Brianna burst in. Marco knew what she was going to say, could tell by the flush on her cheeks and the excitement that shone in her eyes.

"Sorry to interrupt," Brianna gushed then shifted her gaze completely to Marco. "Marco, can you come into the kitchen when you get a chance. I'd like you to do a little taste test."

"I look forward to it."

Leo lifted an eyebrow in question after Brianna shut the door. "What's that all about?"

"Brianna's coming up with some recipe ideas for our latest product."

Leo gave an impressed nod. "Excellent. Now about what you were asking me…"

"Just stay tuned, my friend. Stay tuned."

Marco worked hard to finalize some notes after Leo had left his office. This working from home thing wasn't so bad, after all. He thought there would be many more outside interruptions. But the only interruption to his concentration right now was of his own making. He really ought to just finish up here but was too distracted by the thought of what Brianna might be cooking up in the kitchen.

Her offer this morning to work on recipes for Dirici Foods had pleased him in a way he couldn't have imagined. How in the world had he not thought of such a thing himself?

Because he'd been thoughtless when it came to her from the very beginning. In all fairness, things were so hectic after they'd eloped and moved here that finding ways to keep his new bride occupied had been the last thing on his mind. Right or wrong, it was the truth. He'd had so much on his plate, right in the middle of a big global expansion, the prep it took to get ready for a new baby. And Brianna's pregnancy hadn't been the easiest.

All the more reason he should have thought to be more considerate of her. Even if they had been barely more than strangers.

He shook off the useless thoughts that would do him no good now and clicked open a spreadsheet. If he didn't get these sales projections entered in right now, he may never get around to it. Then he would go and see what concoction Brianna had come up with. He could hardly wait. There was no good to come of wallowing in the mistakes he'd made in the past where his wife was concerned. All he could do was try and take things day by day and find ways to make up for it all. He made quick work of the entries and powered off his laptop. A good start would be to go and try this recipe she was working on.

He found her elbow-deep in pots and pans in the kitchen amidst a cloud of steam. A rich aroma of spices and herbs greeted him.

"Ah, there you are." She gave him a wide smile. "Come here and try this. I feel like it needs something else."

Dipping a large wooden spoon into a saucepan, she held it up to his mouth when he approached.

"Careful, it's really hot."

An explosion of taste erupted on his tongue when he took a bite of what she offered. Sure, she'd cooked for him before but never anything she was experimenting on. This was unlike anything he'd tasted. She'd incorporated the Dirici flavored oil and added some type of pepper. Not really spicy hot but it definitely held a zing.

"It's good."

"Well, don't look so surprised."

The truth was, he sort of was surprised. Not so much at her talent but that she'd come up with something so quickly.

"I'm simply enjoying it, *cara*."

"Well, thank you. I'm glad you like it. I'll have a detailed recipe for you at some point. It still needs some work."

"I can't wait."

"Good. In the meantime, why don't you go wash your hands?"

"What for?"

"If you're in here, you may as well make yourself useful and help me."

For a strange moment, neither one of them said anything, a baited silence hung in there. Then they both burst out laughing. Those were the very same words she'd said to him the first time they'd met, as soon as he'd wandered into the kitchen at the cocktail party he'd been attending and she was catering. It was like being catapulted back in time. And he was every bit as attracted to her now as he was then.

* * *

Finally, Brianna turned back to her pans and started to stir the contents as Marco walked over to the sink and washed his hands.

"Hand me the jar of pepper paste, would you?" she ordered as soon as he was done.

He gasped with mock outrage. "So comfortable ordering me around. Fine, at least I'll have a front row seat to witness your sorcery." He stepped closer to her and lifted her chin with his finger. "But just one thing first."

"What's that?"

"I'd like a taste of something else before we get started."

His gaze fell to her lips and she couldn't help but let out a soft moan. An eternity seemed to pass as she waited. And then his mouth found hers. Sighing with pleasure, she leaned into him, moved her hands up his shoulders. This was Marco; he tasted exotic and new yet oh, so familiar. It was like she'd known him forever and loved him just as long.

Exactly like the first time he'd kissed her.

CHAPTER TEN

BRIANNA SET ENZO down gently into his crib and pulled the soft terry cover over him. As exhausted as he was, it had still taken several bedtime stories to finally get him to fall asleep. She breathed a sigh of relief that he was finally down and stepped into the outer area of the nursery, shutting his bedroom door softly behind her.

What was Marco doing at the moment? He'd surprised her earlier by holding his meeting with Leo at the house. She'd fully expected him to run out and stay gone for at least the rest of the day. But by some miracle, he'd stayed home.

And he'd surprised her even further by helping her cook.

Maybe she'd find her husband now and ask him to join her on the veranda to share an evening drink. They could always discuss some more recipe ideas. Or other subjects for that matter.

But first she had some tidying to do. Enzo's

toys and books were strewn all over the floor. As tempting as it was, Brianna couldn't leave this to deal with the next day. She got to work picking up and putting items away. Shelving the books, Brianna realized they weren't all toddler hardcovers. A few photo albums lay on the floor next to the bedtime fairy tales. Nonna must have brought them in here to look over with Enzo. She remembered the first afternoon they'd come back, Enzo had sat on Nonna's lap as they perused through photos.

She opened one of the albums and flipped through a couple of pages. The first thing that struck her was how much her little boy looked like a younger version of his father. Especially in one particular shot taken of Marco smiling on a small toddler bike. If the photo hadn't looked worn, she'd be hard pressed to say whether it was her son or husband beaming back at her in the image.

After several moments of browsing, she finally got ready to close the album and put it away. But a wayward thought nagged at her. The Dirici home had several shelves of photo albums and there were framed pictures decorating various walls of the house. Yet she'd never seen any pictures of Marco's mother. It was as if the woman had never existed.

How could she have never noticed it before?

She grabbed another photo album and flipped through the pages. Within a few short minutes, she'd gone through every book. None of them held any photos of her whatsoever. In fact, one book was dedicated completely to Marco's birth, with no sign of the woman who'd borne him.

Her eyes started to sting with tears. When exactly had Marco tried to erase the memory of the mother who had abandoned him? As a child? How vulnerable that little boy must have felt, how truly betrayed and alone. Brianna rubbed her eyes and made her way out of the room. She wouldn't say anything to Marco about any of it. Mentioning the curious lack of any images of Marco's mother would no doubt only serve to open old wounds. But how deeply she yearned that he would trust her enough one day to willingly tell her on his own.

Nonna was coming up the stairs as she stepped out into the hall. Brianna managed to summon a smile.

"Are you all right, dear?"

"Yes, I'm fine, Nonna. Thank you."

"It just took a while to get Enzo down," she added when Marie looked less than convinced. "I may have dozed off in the rocking chair myself."

"I see," the older woman replied. Her eyes studied Brianna's face. Marco's grandmother had always been way too perceptive.

"In fact, I think I'll take a quick walk around the gardens to get myself awake."

"I wish I could join you but I'm still feeling somewhat under the weather."

"That's okay." Brianna smiled and started to make her way down the stairs. Then her feet seemed to stop of their own volition before Brianna made it down the first step. She knew it was oh, so stupid what she was about to do. But she couldn't seem to help herself.

Nonna gave her an expectant look. "What is it, dear?"

"I wanted to ask you something. I hope you don't think it sounds gossipy."

The older woman gave her an indulgent smile. "This sounds serious. Ask away."

Brianna sucked in a breath of air. Why was she

doing this? "It's just. I wondered if Marco had heard from his mother. I mean, recently."

"What brought this on?" Nonna asked.

At the question, Brianna felt even more foolish for pursuing the matter. "Never mind, Nonna. Please forget I said anything."

"Nevertheless, the answer is a sad one."

"It is?"

"We received an official letter about three years ago. Notifying us that she had passed. A car accident, it said. A solicitor who was tasked with letting us know."

A rock dropped into Brianna's stomach. "Three years ago?"

Nonna nodded. "That's right. Right before he was due to travel to the States, in fact."

Right before they'd met. Had Marco simply been seeking solace in her arms then? Did he just need a gentle touch? Or worse, a mere distraction?

If true, look at the fundamental changes all of it had led to. For both of them.

"Anything else?" Nonna asked at Brianna's continued silence.

Brianna gave her head a shake. "No. Thank you. I was just curious."

Nonna waited a beat before replying. "I will see you at dinner then, my dear. Enjoy your walk." With that, the older woman turned and made her way toward her own suite of rooms. "I rather feel the need for a quick nap myself."

"I hope you have a good rest, Nonna," Brianna said and managed another forced smile. It didn't come easy.

"I was hoping I would catch you before running into the office today." Marco approached the counter where Brianna stood pouring herself her first cup of coffee of the morning. She'd had a restless night, tossing and turning.

She turned to him with her mug to her lips. "You're going in today? On a Saturday?"

He fixed a cuff link on his left wrist. He looked impeccable. In a steel-gray tailored suit and sky-blue tie, Marco was every inch the successful business tycoon. "I've got some sales meetings with consultants flying in from all over Europe. This was the only date that worked."

She couldn't resist reaching up and straightening his tie clip, though it was nowhere near askew enough that anyone else would probably have even noticed. Standing next to him, in her rumpled flannel robe with her hair all tangled, she must have looked like the lowly peasant standing next to the regal prince.

Why couldn't she be one of those women who went to bed in silk flimsy nighties with matching covers?

Brianna blinked away the thought. "What did you want to see me about?"

Marco reached behind her for a cup but he turned to the silver carafe which held fresh brewed espresso. How he and Nonna could drink such harsh brew first thing was a mystery to her. He started to drink it straight.

"Leo reminded me of the regatta happening next week."

"The one you had to miss last year?" He'd had to miss it because Enzo had come down with an ear infection and the resulting temperature readings had alarmed them both. Marco hadn't attended the year before either, that time due to Enzo's recent arrival.

"Yes, that's the one."

"What about it?"

He set his cup down on the counter. "Why don't you come with me? We can make a trip of it."

She hadn't seen that offer coming. "Won't you be racing?"

"Yes. But it's so much more than just a race. There'll be festival activities. Not to mention some of the best Italian cuisine this side of the country."

"It sounds amazing."

"It is. Every port along the fifteen-mile coast of the race has something special to partake in. I think you'd enjoy it."

"What about Enzo?"

He tapped her nose playfully. "I have a full staff here. Not to mention, he has a very capable Nonna at his very disposal."

Brianna mulled it over. She'd never been on so much as a harbor cruise let alone on an actual sailing expedition.

And this was a big part of Marco's life. He'd always been an avid boater. Here he was, asking her to share that part of him. She'd be hard pressed to turn it down.

"He has been sleeping through the night since

we got here." She glanced toward the ceiling in the direction of her son's bedroom. In fact, he was still asleep at the moment. "I would hate to do anything to set him back though."

"Why don't you think about it?" he told her, clearly dismissing the subject. "I take it you'll be working on some more recipes today?" A small spark of disappointment settled in her chest. He obviously wasn't terribly invested in the idea of her accompanying him given the way he was ready to change the topic.

She nodded. "Yes, I have some more ideas about what other ingredients I might add to that last dish."

"Excellent. I'll be very late tonight." He grabbed his case off the ground and walked out of the kitchen. Moments later, Brianna heard the roar of his engine. There was no question she wouldn't be seeing him again today. Not with the workday he'd just described.

She wanted to kick herself. Why had she even hesitated rather than simply accepting his invitation?

What if he didn't ask again?

* * *

Marco gripped the steering wheel of his late-model Lamborghini and slowly pulled down the mansion's long, winding driveway.

She needed to think about it. About whether she wanted to accompany him to the regatta. The notion was somewhat demoralizing. His own wife needed to consider before agreeing to a week spent sailing along the coast with him.

They'd never done such a thing before. In fact, they hadn't even gone on a proper honeymoon. There hadn't been time or opportunity given the pregnancy and complications. The regatta would give them an opportunity to finally spend some time together. Alone. Maybe even get to know each other a bit better.

But Brianna hadn't jumped at the prospect. She had a solid reason, her concern about being away from Enzo. Marco knew he was being silly. Downright immature. What was it about his own wife that brought out that unflattering side of him? He just couldn't help but feel somewhat slighted that she hadn't seemed more…well, excited about the whole prospect.

He turned onto the road and tried to focus on

the day that was ahead. The meetings before him were way too important to let his focus scatter in any way.

She hadn't said no. He supposed he should be happy for that much at least.

CHAPTER ELEVEN

MARCO WASN'T USED to waiting. Particularly not having to wait for Brianna. The woman had always been prompt and timely since he'd met her. For some reason, she was taking an annoyingly long time this morning.

But then she stepped out into the sunshine and he couldn't think at all. He could barely breathe. In a light, flowy sundress that hung on her curves with precision, she looked like a Roman princess.

And her hair. She'd done something differently; her curls were tamer, secured at the base of her neck with a few soft tendrils framing her face.

Correction, she looked like a Roman goddess.

All in all, what she wore appeared to be a very reasonable, even sensible uniform for a day of intense sailing. But for some reason it looked far from that. In fact, it was knocking the sense right out of him.

"Is something wrong?" Her voice shook as she asked the question. He'd been blatantly staring at her.

He could only manage to clear his throat.

"I could go change if this isn't appropriate," she added, again with hesitation in her tone and rubbing her hands down her sides.

"Don't you dare."

She blinked at him, confusion etched in her features.

"I mean, that's perfect. What you have on will work great."

Relief flooded her face. "Thanks. Nonna helped me pick it out."

He made a mental note to thank Nonna profusely as soon as they got back home from this trip.

"I've never done anything like this before. I wasn't quite sure what to pick out," she added.

Marco felt guilty at that comment. "I must apologize for that. I should have found a way to get you on the boat."

She stepped up to him, placed her palm against his chest. "Oh, no. Don't apologize. I was in no mood to go sailing when we first arrived in Italy.

And once Enzo was born, there was hardly time to eat or sleep, let alone do anything leisurely."

Her words served to lighten his guilt somewhat. But he couldn't shake the feeling that if he'd really wanted to, he would have figured out a way to take her. He would have found a way to share that part of his life with her. Among other things.

He guided her to the passenger seat of the sports car. Then he threw their bags in the back.

"We'll be at the marina in just a few minutes," he told her as they headed off. In no time, they were driving along the coast and traffic increased exponentially. The race always drew a great amount of people to the area. Observers as well as other sailors.

They reached the entrance to the marina and seemingly had to wait an exorbitant amount of time before being able to park. Once they did, it was a small walk to the Dirici slip.

Marco guided Brianna onboard while a porter carried and deposited their bags. Despite the strange circumstances surrounding this trip—an attempt to get to know better a woman he was already married to—he finally, slowly felt himself begin to relax. Being on deck with the sunshine, the refreshing breeze, and anticipatory hum in the air before a big race had the usual effect of settling his soul.

Brianna for her part appeared in awe. "This is what you called your small sailing boat?"

"Do you like it?"

Brianna ran a hand along the rail. "It's gorgeous. And it's hardly a sailboat. It's more like a yacht!"

Marco felt an almost giddy satisfaction that his craft had impressed her so. How childish and silly was that?

"Not really. Just a fifty-foot sailboat with an inboard engine. Serves me fine. I've had it for several years." He hadn't had time to do much on it for the past couple of years though. He found he was very much looking forward to the competition tomorrow.

He'd never actually stopped to think about exactly how much had changed in his life during such a short span.

Marco motioned for Brianna to follow him below deck. "Here, I'll show you the living quarters."

When they got below, Brianna's jaw seemed to drop even lower. "This is almost a mini apartment."

He laughed. "Well, the tour won't take long." He pointed straight in front of him. "Kitchen, bed, and the bathroom is to your left."

Was it his imagination, or had Brianna's eyes lingered on the bed for just an instant before looking away? He found himself focused on it as well, his mind wandering to what the night would entail as they shared it.

He turned before his body could react any further. Taking Brianna by the elbow, he led her to the mini fridge. "Can I get you something to drink? There's chilled wine, soda. Or water if you prefer."

"I don't dare have wine on an empty stomach." She clapped her hands. "Oh, that reminds me. I made some sandwiches for us. They're in an insulated bag in my luggage. Would you care for one now?"

As thoughtful as that was, this regatta was just as much about the food as it was the actual race. He should have been clearer. "You didn't need to trouble yourself. There'll be food and drinks at every stop."

Her smile deflated before he spoke the last

word and Marco wanted to kick himself. He should have just eaten whatever she'd prepared. But they had plans at the very next stop for a meal. Again, something he should have shared with her much sooner.

"I just thought we might get hungry before…"

"No, as I said it was a very kind and thoughtful gesture. But I didn't get a chance to mention that we have plans to eat at the next stop."

"We do?"

He nodded. "Some friends are meeting us. We'll be getting there just in time for an early evening dinner. I apologize for not telling you sooner."

She waved her hand in dismissal. "Don't be silly. I'm a chef, eating at new establishments is a thrill for me."

Her words didn't seem to match her tone. He detected a subtle yet clear hint of disappointment.

"You know, I think I am kind of hungry," he lied. "I'll have a quick bite after all. It will be close to an hour before we eat, now that I think about it."

He moved to go retrieve her bag with the sandwiches when she stopped him. "Uh-uh. No way. As a professional, I will not let you spoil your appetite before a five-star restaurant meal."

"No, really—" he began to protest.

"It's okay, Marco. We'll just save the sand-wiches for another time. I'm just going to freshen up." She turned without another word and stepped into bathroom.

Such a silly misunderstanding, Marco thought, watching her retreat.

He would make it up to her somehow. He re-fused to let something as trivial as uneaten sand-wiches mar this trip before it had even started.

She was so clueless.

Brianna rummaged in her bag for her lip gloss in the small stately bathroom of Marco's boat. What a simpleton. She'd made sandwiches. Like they were going off on some picnic. A true fish out of water, Brianna Stedman was. Her last name might be Dirici now but in her bones she was still southern New Jersey. Girls like her didn't real-ize that sailboats could be this large or have liv-ing quarters this luxurious. She wasn't sure what she'd been expecting but it certainly hadn't been anything this elaborate.

The earth moved under her feet. Brianna

grabbed the edge of the sink to steady herself. They must be departing.

She'd spent so much time picking out exactly what to wear, so much time on getting her hair just right. At least all that effort seemed to have paid off. Marco looked appreciative when he'd first laid eyes on her earlier today. In fact, the look he'd given her had sent heat curling through her stomach.

She just wished she was a bit more worldly. Heavens, she'd never even been on a boat before. Unless you counted paddleboarding on the Jersey shore. This was a large part of Marco's life. She wanted to understand it more. She wanted to be part of it. But it was completely alien to her.

She would have to shape up. And she would have to do it quickly. They were to meet people in a few short moments. And she didn't want to give the impression that she didn't know what she was doing or how to behave.

Marco's friends would be cut from the same elite cloth that he was. European upper class.

She studied her face in the mirror and almost had to laugh. How had she ended up here? She was in Italy on the Amalfi coast with her billionaire husband on his yacht before a race.

No, not a race. A *regatta*.

If someone had suggested such a thing to the young adult she was a few short years ago she would have laughed in their face. Actually, she would have been too tired to laugh, between long hours at culinary school and putting herself through it by working odd, low-paying jobs.

Her present predicament was certainly a far cry from where that young lady had been. She'd ended up in a completely different universe without even really knowing how it had happened. At first she'd simply been too focused on her new baby boy to really acknowledge all the changes that were happening to her life. But there was no denying, Brianna Stedman was a totally different person in a totally different world.

The few short years in between felt like they could have been an entire lifetime.

So how come the reflection staring back at her now from the mirror taunted that nothing about her had really changed at all?

CHAPTER TWELVE

SHE COULDN'T ALLOW herself to be sick.

Brianna leaned over the rail and stared at the water below. They were about half a mile from the coast from what she could tell, traveling at a steady speed. The blue-green of the sea was broken by white-capped foam where the boat's hull met the water.

Every once in a while she caught Marco's eye as he stood steering at the helm. She gave him a tentative smile and gripped the railing tighter. Her legs felt wobbly but she didn't dare sit. She didn't dare move. Her stomach insisted on doing queasy flips. Her throat burned with acidic bile. This was so much worse than any bout of morning sickness she could remember. And this wasn't even the race yet, they were simply cruising to their first destination.

So this was what seasickness felt like. As if

Brianna needed any more proof that she was utterly out of her element.

Marco appeared oblivious to her discomfort. Hopefully, she'd be able to keep it that way. With any luck, it would all go away once she got something solid in her stomach. Though the thought of food immediately made her stomach go from a minor flip to an all-out heave.

She gripped the steel rail so tight her knuckles turned white. What had she been thinking? She could be back at the mansion right now, rocking her little boy to sleep with her feet on solid ground.

What seemed like an eternity later, Marco seemed to pull in toward land and maneuver around several other crafts. Brianna closed her eyes and willed her body to behave. She heard the engine shut off finally and then Marco's footsteps approaching behind her.

That had to have been the longest hour of her life.

"We're here."

She turned to face him and was struck momentarily by his wide grin. His cheeks glowed a healthy red, a bright twinkle in his eyes. Unlike her, he'd apparently enjoyed every minute of their ride.

"The coastline looked beautiful," she managed to mutter.

His brow suddenly furrowed and the grin disappeared into a tight frown. "Are you all right?" he asked with concern. "You're looking a little pale."

She forced her mouth into a smile. "I'm fine. Must have been the wind blowing in my face."

Marco hesitated and studied her some more. Brianna bit the inside of her cheek to keep from gagging. Hard.

"Are you sure? You're not seasick, are you?"

She made herself shake her head, the effort resulting in a nasty pounding in her temple. At least morning sickness had never involved headaches.

"No, not at all." What a talent she had that she'd never known about! Being able to lie so blatantly even while feeling this miserable. "Shall we go then? Meet these friends of yours?" Holding on to Marco's arm, she made her feet move. If he noticed how tight her grip was, he didn't let on.

Stepping on dry land only offered minimal comfort. The marina was crowded and noisy. Someone was playing Italian opera at a high decibel from a nearby speaker. A group of teen girls jostled her as they rushed by. Brianna found herself shoved close to Marco's side and for a horrifying moment she thought she might lose her control and be sick over his arm.

Taking a deep breath, she tried to steady herself.

"There they are," Marco said above her ear.

Brianna looked up to see a group of well-heeled people about twenty feet away, right by the water. They sat around a metal table at some sort of outdoor café; two opened bottles of wine seemed to have been casualties already. Three women and two men. A laughing Leo sat right at the center, sipping from a long-stemmed glass. Brianna felt a small hint of relief. At least there was one familiar face amongst them.

"Let's go," Marco said and gently fought their way through the crowd toward the group. Brianna forced back yet another surge of bile at the base of her throat.

One of the ladies looked up just as they approached. She was stunning, so much so that Brianna missed a step. She regained her footing and just barely avoided crashing face-first into the chest of a passing stranger.

Brianna shut her eyes tight and said a small prayer. Maybe when she opened them again she would realize she'd overestimated the woman's beauty.

The prayer went unanswered. The vision before her had to be some type of model or actress. The other females at the table also held their own in the looks department.

Brianna ran her hand through her unruly curls. No amount of primping would put her on par with the likes of the ladies before her right now.

Leo stood as soon as he spotted them and pulled two nearby chairs to their table. "There they are," his voice boomed through the air. "The lovely Brianna and her boor of a husband."

Marco replied with some type of hand gesture Brianna didn't understand. Definitely not anything she'd seen in New York. Leo only laughed louder.

Any other time and she would have laughed at the men's humorous banter. Right now, it was taking all she had to simply stand straight. Between shock and nausea, it was proving to be quite a battle. So not the first impression she was shooting for with Marco's friends.

Marco guided her to the table as laughter and mock cheers greeted them. Brianna managed a weak wave but didn't dare try to speak. Opening her mouth would be too risky. The brunette stood and gave Marco a kiss. Only on the cheek but it was definitely a lingering one. She said something to him in Italian and Marco barked out in laughter. Brianna slammed a hand against her belly. Her stomach had gone from flips to all-out gymnastic level cartwheels.

Finally, the brunette turned and directed the focus of her shapely, dark eyes right on her. High cheekbones, dark eyes, a pert nose. The woman could have been an image straight out of a painting, the descendant of a Renaissance portrait subject.

She addressed her in English with a heavy accent and a warm smile. "I'm Natalia, but I'm called Talia."

The woman continued speaking but Brianna could hear nothing through the roaring suddenly echoing in her ears. The world started to shift around her and then it began to spin.

There was nothing for it. She couldn't even pretend anymore. She was going to be sick.

"Excuse me," she managed to blurt out and

turned on her heel. Covering her mouth with the back of her hand, she tried to put as much distance between herself and the group as possible.

She barely made it to the edge of the water in time.

What kind of man didn't know his wife had never been on a boat before?

Marco could simply stare as Brianna shoved past him and hurled herself through the crowd. He lost sight of her for a split second in the bustling sea of people. When he spotted her again he bit out a sharp curse in Italian. She stood bent over by the edge of the water. Violently ill.

"Scusa," he said to his shocked friends and made his way over to where his wife stood.

"Brianna?"

She lifted a hand but didn't turn to look at him. "Please, Marco. Just leave me alone."

How was he supposed to do that? What did she expect? For him to just walk away and hope she didn't pass out or anything? "Uh, can I get you some water? Or ice?"

Her response was another heave. He reached

for her tentatively before dropping his hand back down by his side.

"Is there any chance you'll walk away?" she asked between what sounded like several violent hiccups.

"Probably not."

This time the response was an elongated groan. So much for showing Brianna a fun time today. He'd failed miserably. It hadn't even occurred to him that she might have an issue on the water. He'd grown up on the water, had been sailing since his teens. He and his grandfather had spent hours cruising along the coast every weekend before the man had passed away several years back.

"I wish there was something I could do for you, *cara*."

She shook her head and wiped her mouth. Marco signaled to a passing vendor selling various ice smoothies. Fortunately, the man also had bottled water. Marco paid the man quickly then held the plastic bottle in Brianna's direction. It took her a minute to notice he was holding something to her. She took it with a shaky hand then brought it to her forehead.

"I'll be all right in a few minutes. Luckily, I hadn't eaten much of anything."

"Yes, you appear quite lucky at the moment," he quipped in an attempt at comic relief.

She didn't appear to be in the mood. All he got was a grimace in response. "I'm so sorry about this, *cara*," he told her.

"Why in the world are you apologizing to me?"

"This trip was my idea. You are my responsibility."

She gave him an incredulous look. "I was the one who got ill in the middle of meeting your friends for the first time ever."

"You can't blame yourself for not being accustomed to the water. I should have thought to take precautions."

She turned to face him fully then. Marco tried not to react to the way she looked. Her pallor had gone completely ashen, dark smudges framed the area beneath her eyes. Her hair had escaped its noose and fell haphazardly around her face and neck.

Somehow, she still looked stunningly beautiful. He shook his head to clear it. What a fanciful thought. They had more pressing matters than how Brianna looked after an episode of seasickness.

"I'm your wife, Marco. Please don't call me your responsibility."

Where had that come from?

He hadn't meant it the way she seemed to be interpreting the statement. For the first time since he'd met her, Marco entertained the possibility that they might have some kind of a language issue between them. They did after all have different first tongues. "I simply meant—"

She held up a hand to stop him. "Please, not now. I just need another minute."

Marco shut his mouth before he could say anything more to upset her. Not only was she not feeling well, she was angry. At him. But she didn't want to hear him apologizing for her predicament. So what was she upset with him about? Brianna turned back and stared at the horizon. He stood silently as she did her best to collect herself. Glancing back to where his friends stood watching them with concern, he gave a reassuring wave.

This trip was turning out nothing like the way he'd imagined.

* * *

The scene at the marina still tugged at her mind though they'd gotten back three days ago. Brianna had toughed it out through the rest of the trip, refusing to return home or letting Marco pull out of the competition.

But she hadn't enjoyed a moment of it. And something had definitely shifted between them afterward. Their brief interlude of a makeshift truce had faded to one of tension and underlying strife. Now, she was moving forward with the decision she'd come to even before their return from the regatta.

Correction, it was the same decision she had made over six months ago when she'd left Italy in the first place. She and Marco belonged to two different worlds. And they definitely didn't belong together.

Marco had been in emotional pain when they'd met. Grieving for his lost mother, whether he'd known it or not. It was only that pain and confusion that had led him into her arms. His anguished state of mind had played the only role in the way he'd behaved that week when they'd first met. What were the chances someone like him would have otherwise even glanced in her direction?

She glanced down at the list of names she'd researched. Names of renowned child psychologists in the Amalfi area. A couple were located as far away as Rome. If she had to, she would make the trip. It was time to get Enzo evaluated, not only to make sure he was thriving, but also to ensure he adjusted properly to the inevitable. His parents weren't going to be a couple that stayed together.

The next step after that would be to try and contact Chef Ziyad again. She had to pursue that possible avenue of employment harder than she'd been able to back in New York.

She didn't know how long any of that would take. But she wasn't going to put it any of it off any longer.

She'd tried, she really had.

Brianna bit back a sob as she reached for the phone to call the first professional on her list. This was so much worse than when she and Marco had failed the first time.

Marco chose that moment to walk in through

the front door. His expression was guarded, his demeanor stiff. Things had been that way between them since they'd gotten back. Even now, as she took in his tailored suit, his coal-dark hair, she had to resist the urge to run into his arms and ask him to kiss her.

How foolish she could be when it came to this man.

"Where's Enzo?" he asked without so much as a hello.

"Nonna took him out by the pond."

He nodded, seemed to look her over. "I'll be in the study for most of the evening. I'll take my dinner in there when it's ready."

"I wanted to talk to you for a moment first."

"Can it wait? I've got a lot to get through before a staff meeting tomorrow."

"I'm afraid I'd rather not delay." She stood before he could get far. Better to just get this over with. "Before you hole up, there are some things we need to go over."

"Hole up? That's how you're going to describe me trying to get some work done?"

Really? That was the battle he wanted to pursue at the moment? Wait till she told him what she'd spent the afternoon doing. "It's just a figure of speech, Marco."

He dropped his briefcase to the ground and rubbed his forehead. "Very well. What is it that you'd like to discuss?"

For an insane moment, Brianna had an urge to voice the questions she really wanted to ask him. If he'd ever thought he might have genuine feelings for the woman he'd inadvertently ended up married to. Despite the unconventional way they'd met, despite the inner turmoil that had led him into her arms.

She cleared her throat. "I've been doing some research since we returned."

"What kind of research?"

"Experts in child rearing."

"I see." He crossed his arms in front of his chest.

"I'd like to get Enzo analyzed. By a child psychologist."

"Has something happened?" A flash of concern flickered in his eyes.

"No. He's actually been a happy, well-adjusted toddler since we returned."

He lifted an eyebrow. "Then I don't see the point."

Brianna let out a deep breath. Yes, he did. Of course he saw the point. He was just going to insist on making her say it, to make her admit her motives out loud.

"I'm trying to think of the long term."

"You're looking for reassurance that it will be okay to take him away again. I thought we'd already had this conversation."

"But we never resolved it. You and I both know this isn't going to work, Marco. We gave it another go. It's not like we didn't."

"Perhaps you're right."

"I am?"

"If you're going to be this temperamental about living here then maybe it will be easier to just make a clean break once and for all." He stepped forward and lifted a finger accusingly. "But I will not have my son adversely affected. We'll see what your experts have to say about any of that."

His words and his whole attitude stoked her

temper. She'd wanted so badly to discuss all this with him in a calm and mature manner. She should have known better. "I know what they're going to say. That children are never better off in the long term if the parents aren't happy in their marriage."

"Is this about the race?" Marco sighed and pinched the bridge of his nose. "Look, I'm sorry you had a miserable time. I'm sorry I made you go."

Did he honestly think that was what her decision was about? The events of that day had simply been the trigger that made their incompatibility glaringly obvious. Yet again.

"It's about so much more than the race."

"Right. It's about being stuck in an unhappy marriage and incompatibility."

He may as well have added *blah, blah, blah* to the end of his statement.

Brianna fought the urge to stomp her foot like a child. "No, more so about how we're from completely different worlds and backgrounds. And you have no interest in trying to address any of that."

"I was the one who asked you to go to the regatta, remember?"

"Yes, and I appreciate the attempt." She inhaled a deep breath as her voice shook. "But how could you have thought it would be enough? I need more than a day boating with you, Marco. I need you to talk to me."

She'd known this wasn't going to be easy. Trying to get through to Marco about her concerns never was.

"What exactly is it that you want me to say, Brianna?"

She wanted him to tell her that it would all right. That he was ready to share his life with her. She wanted to hear that he would never doubt their future together. For the sake of her child and her heart, she wanted that guarantee.

But she knew that would all be asking too much. Sooner or later, it would all turn for the worse.

Maybe not tomorrow, maybe not next week. But it was a certainty. Why had she ever thought she could fit in with the likes of Marco Dirici?

He was yachting and vineyards and international corporate offices.

He'd only turned to her during a time of torment and confusion after finding out his estranged mother had died after abandoning him years before. If not for his shock and certain anger, he probably wouldn't have given someone like Brianna Stedman the time of day.

After all, she was nothing more than a cook from New Jersey.

CHAPTER THIRTEEN

MARCO LOOSENED HIS tie and shrugged off his jacket. With all the frustration and agitation he was feeling, he threw them onto the sofa. Then he wished he had something else to throw, something that would break and shatter. His wife stood in front of him like a small waif facing a royal guard. Under any other circumstances, he might actually admire her determination.

Everything had gone so wrong. He wished he'd never entered that godforsaken regatta. Then maybe Brianna wouldn't be looking at him right now like a wasp she wanted to swat away. He'd expected too much, put too much faith in one little trip. A foolish part of him thought he and Brianna would be returning from the coast with a renewed sense of solidarity and family. The exact opposite had occurred.

Instead, she was telling him she wanted to leave again.

Served him right for having such ridiculous thoughts in the first place. Did he think one sailing trip was going to make any kind of difference? If he hadn't been able to make his wife care for him after all this time, what did that say about the kind of man he was? To think, he'd ridiculed his own father for so many years for essentially the same thing.

"I again have to ask, what exactly would you like me to say, *cara*?"

A brief flash of emotion flickered in her eyes. He didn't have it in him to try and analyze it. Not now.

She clasped her hands in front of her belly and for an insane moment he wanted to reach out to her. He wanted to take those hands into his and bring them to his mouth. To tell her that things would be all right. That they would figure it all out. That they had to try for the sake of their son. He almost took a step forward in her direction before he caught himself.

"You have nothing you would like to say?"

"Not a thing I can think of."

She seemed to deflate like a balloon before his very eyes. "I have no choice then. I'd like to move forward with my plans to have Enzo seen by a professional. Would you like to provide any input?"

"As far as?"

She wrung her hands tighter. "About the doctor we take Enzo to. About how to prep him for the return to New York. I'm sure we should go over some of this together."

We?

She was serious. Did she honestly expect him to help further the process along under these circumstances? Did she not see that he felt totally cut off at the knees? "I really have no interest in any of that. Like you said, *cara*. These are all *your* plans."

"But don't you—?"

Marco was done listening. He dismissed her by turning away and then picked his briefcase off the floor. "Update me as necessary. I have work to do."

Brianna let him go without further argument. He didn't know whether to be relieved or disappointed.

Marco closed the door to his study and walked over to the large window overlooking the south lawn. This scene always soothed him. The pathway that led to Nonna's precious gardens, the rolling hills in the distance. It was one of the reasons he had chosen this room as his at-home office. For the sense of calm this view provided him.

But not today.

He'd let her down. He'd placed Brianna in a predicament and environment she was utterly unprepared for. And then he'd been unable to help in any way.

Biting out a curse, he grabbed the glass paperweight off his desk and got ready to throw it against the wall. A rapid knock on the door stopped him midthrow.

"Come in."

Brianna had followed him. Her gaze fell to the paperweight Marco still gripped viselike in his hands. But she didn't comment on it. "I'd like to continue discussing this."

Marco set the paperweight down as Brianna stepped into the room and shut the door behind her.

"I already apologized for taking you sailing, Brianna."

She gave an exasperated huff. "You think that's what this is about?"

"What else? You must blame me for not realizing you would get sick."

"That's a ridiculous notion, Marco. It's not your fault I got sick."

"Maybe not directly." The truth was, he should have at least asked her about her past experiences on the water.

"Or indirectly," she countered. "I got sick because I've never really been on a boat before. But my husband's an avid sailor."

He blinked. "Is there supposed to be some kind of logic behind that statement? A metaphor perhaps?"

She slammed her hands against her hips. "The fact is I'm completely out of my element here at times. I don't really know what I'm doing."

She was clearly referring to more than just being on a boat. "You're saying we're not a good match."

"Can you deny it?" she demanded to know. "We never would have even gotten married if it wasn't for Enzo."

He studied her. She seemed absolutely certain of what she'd just said. "You can be so sure?"

His question shocked her, as if she'd never really entertained an alternate possibility.

"If that's wrong. Then why?"

"Why what?"

"Why are you so distant? So guarded? You refuse to open up to me about anything. Not even what you were dealing with that week we met."

So she'd found out about his mother and the news he'd gotten right before traveling to the States that first time.

But before Marco could come up with a response, they were interrupted by a sharp knock on the door.

It was Carlo; he'd gone deathly pale. "Signore Marco, come quick. It's your grandmother."

"What happened?" Marco demanded to know as she chased behind him to Marie's suite. Brianna's heart thudded in her chest at the thought of what they might find.

"I don't know exactly," Carlo answered then followed up with something else in Italian.

Marco barked something in response to the

other man who quickly turned and dashed the other way down the hallway. Presumably to call medical attention, Brianna figured.

When they got to her suite, Nonna didn't appear at all well. She was breathing heavily, her skin the color of ash. Marco immediately ran to her side and crouched down next to her.

"Nonna? Can you speak?"

Marie made a futile attempt to brush away his concern with a wave of her hand. "I'm fine. Just trying to catch my breath. I must have overdone it in the gardens earlier."

Brianna's mouth had gone dry. Whatever was happening to Marco's grandmother appeared to be much more than simple overexertion.

"I'm sure it is." Marco was trying to reassure her. "But we're going to have you checked out just in case, okay?"

Nonna made an attempt to sit up, then gave up and settled back into the cushion. "That's just silly. I wish you hadn't called them."

Brianna uttered a silent prayer of thanks that Enzo was asleep and not around to see his great-grandmother in such a state. She was having enough trouble taking in the scene herself. Nonna had never been anything less than formidable since Brianna had first laid eyes on her.

Marco took his grandmother's hand, whispered softly to her in Italian. Brianna's eyes began to sting. He looked so tender, so concerned. Nonna had been the one to bring him up, more a mother to him than his actual parent. Brianna didn't want to imagine what it would do to Marco if he lost her.

Finally, after what seemed to be an eternity, they heard the sirens outside.

The next few minutes went by in a blur. A team of medics fitted Nonna with an oxygen mask, started checking various vitals, and then carried her down the stairs. Brianna didn't even realize it, but at some point she'd reached for Marco's arm with both hands and was holding on to it tight.

"I'm going to go with her," he told her as they watched Nonna being carried away.

He started to pull free but Brianna didn't loosen her grasp. "If you don't mind, I'd like to come with you."

He nodded once then turned and looked at her for the first time since she'd summoned him earlier. His eyes held such apprehension, such downright fear. For one surreal moment, she imagined she might be looking at Enzo after a particularly nasty nightmare. Her strong, formidable husband looked anything but. Right now, he looked like a scared little boy.

Brianna thought her heart might break at the thought.

"I'd like that," he told her.

CHAPTER FOURTEEN

MARCO WATCHED BRIANNA just outside the emergency clinic entrance as she spoke into her cell phone. She was calling to check on Enzo. A glance at his own device told him it was almost 10:00 p.m. They had pulled Nonna out once more about twenty minutes ago to run yet more tests. He'd never been a terribly patient man, and waiting for such long durations under these circumstances was just about driving him *pazza*.

Brianna stepped through the doors and made her way back to the seat next to him. "Violetta says Enzo is still asleep. The sirens and all the activity didn't even stir him."

"Good. That's good."

"Everyone back at the mansion is terribly concerned. Violetta bombarded me with questions. I tried to tell her we just don't know much yet."

Marco rubbed a hand down his face and tried to focus on her words. He hated this clinic. Though it had gone through several renovations over the past few years, the overall setting and the pungent smell of antiseptic hadn't changed.

"I told them Nonna's personal doctor was here," Brianna was saying. "That he was nice enough to come in to oversee her procedures. That seemed to reassure everyone somewhat."

"Yes. Dr. Gia is also a dear friend."

"Did he mention Nonna having issues recently?"

Marco shook his head. "No, in fact he appeared as shocked as the rest of us. Nonna had just recently been in for a routine physical and he declared her fit as an ox."

"Let's hope that means this isn't anything terribly serious."

Marco rested his elbows on his knees. He suddenly felt beyond tired, utterly weary. Brianna edged closer to him. Hesitantly, she reached for his hand. He let her take it then squeezed his fingers around her small palm. He allowed himself to just breathe for a moment and enjoy the warmth of her touch. They were the only two people in the waiting area. A family of four with a crying baby had left within the hour. For several moments, neither of them bothered to speak.

"I'm glad you're here, *cara*," he finally admitted. She had no idea how much he meant it. Being here a little over a decade ago was one of the worst experiences of his existence.

"I wasn't going to make you wait for word here alone, Marco."

"The last time I was alone."

She turned to him. He felt her studying his profile. "The last time?"

"My father was rushed here several years ago before being lifted to the main hospital in the city. Nonna and Nonno were away in Greece for a family wedding. I was the only one to accompany Papa when he fell ill. He never made it back home."

"Oh, Marco." She sighed his name and he felt her soft breath against his cheek. "How old were you?"

"Barely nineteen. I hadn't started university yet."

"That's an awfully young age to not have either parent."

He shrugged. "Maybe. But in truth I'd lost the

better part of him long before that. Twelve years before to be exact."

"When your mother left."

"They may as well both have left that day. I never got my real father back after that. If he was ever really there to begin with. He just couldn't seem to recover from her loss."

"A broken heart can be impossible to recover from for some people."

Marco studied the tile between his feet. It had been scrubbed to a high shine. Was that the same tile he'd stared at ten years ago? Or had it been one of the things that had been changed? He'd tried hard not to think about those hours he'd spent worried and scared. He'd wondered if he should try to find his mother. To tell her what was happening to the husband she'd deserted. But he hadn't had a clue where to start to try and locate her.

"A broken heart coupled with the sting of betrayal." He rubbed his eyes. "I think it's actually what killed him. Slowly. He ignored his responsibilities at Dirici Foods. The company suffered terrible losses for months until Nonno took over the reins again. And Nonna was sharp enough to realize the same neglect was probably being suffered by his child."

He'd never spoken of these things. Not even to Nonna. Definitely not to any other woman. Had no idea why he was doing so now.

But it felt good to have her next to him, to feel her soft skin against his. And to know that whatever the doctors came out to tell him, she would be there with him when they did. So he let himself continue.

"I blamed myself that night," he told her. "Felt consumed with guilt."

"I don't understand. Why would you feel that way?"

"Because maybe the demands of a child had been too much for her to deal with. Maybe she would have stayed if it wasn't for me and he would have remained the vibrant, happy man he'd once been."

"But you were just a child."

"I know. It made no sense. And then I blamed myself for not trying harder to find her when I was older. Maybe if I had just convinced her to at least see him again before he'd gotten sick." He sighed.

She leaned into him; he could smell the lavender scent of her shampoo. It had a soothing effect on his frazzled nerves. Whether it was the scent or her closeness he didn't even know. Nor did he care. He was just grateful.

"You asked me earlier this evening about being guarded."

He heard her suck in a breath. "Yes?"

"You're right. I was so afraid of becoming like my father—losing control of his whole grip on life—all because of an ill-fated relationship. I did everything in my power to avoid it at all costs."

Brianna didn't respond. Just nuzzled closer into his shoulder. He found himself leaning into her as well.

That's how Dr. Gia found them an hour and a half later.

She'd somehow dozed off. Brianna jolted awake when Marco suddenly gripped her shoulders then stood. The doctor was approaching from the patient area down the corridor. Marco strode to meet him halfway with Brianna fast on his heels.

"Sorry to keep you waiting, Marco," Dr. Gia said as they reached him. A short thin man with kind eyes and silver-gray hair, he had a soft soothing voice that must have served him well given his profession. "You can breathe easy. She's stabilized now and breathing without the aid of an oxygen mask."

Marco blew out a loud sigh. His shoulders visibly dropped.

"The better news is that there appear to be no signs of a cardiac event."

"Oh, thank God," Brianna said, and a surge of relief nearly had her knees wobbling beneath her.

"Then what caused all this?" Marco demanded.

The doctor pulled off his glasses and started wiping them with his lab coat. "Her blood pressure when she came in has me quite concerned. She responded to the medication given to lower it. But it's still not anywhere near within normal parameters."

"What could have possibly caused that?" Marco wanted to know.

"That's what we'll need to figure out. But it certainly could have caused the shortness of breath and the heart palpitations."

"I see. May we take her home?"

"Yes. She's free to go. But I want to see her

tomorrow. There are some lifestyle changes we need to discuss. And that blood pressure needs to be monitored going forward."

"Lifestyle changes?" Brianna asked.

"I'm afraid Signora Dirici's days of Gusto espresso are over," Dr. Gia declared with finality.

"You'll have to be the one to tell her," Marco told him with a smile that didn't quite reach his eyes.

By the time they got Nonna home and tucked into her bed, Brianna felt like she'd run a half marathon. Between holding herself so tense as they'd awaited news and the hard plastic chairs in the waiting room, her body actually ached. She and Marco had parted ways at Nonna's suite when he'd gone to reassure the staff who had stayed awake to hear about her condition. Brianna had sworn she could hear their sighs of relief all the way up on the second floor as she'd been checking on Enzo.

As tired as she was, she knew she wasn't going to get any sleep. The adrenaline surge of the past few hours wouldn't abate any time soon. She made her way to the kitchen. Her throat felt dry and scratchy and Violetta always kept fresh lemonade on hand.

She found Marco standing in front of the fridge with the door open. The kitchen was dark save for the small lightbulb in the door of the appliance. For a moment she could do nothing but stare. He still wore his suit pants and work shirt. His sleeves were rolled up and his hands were jammed into his pockets. Brianna's heart lurched in her chest. He'd been so worried about his grandmother. And when she thought about the things he had confided in her, she wanted to weep for the young man who'd had to grow up way too soon.

What would he do if she gave in to the urge to go wrap her arms around him? Would he turn around and reciprocate? So much had happened between them in such a short amount of time. She honestly didn't know how he would react to any kind of gesture right now. Yes, he'd been very open at the clinic. But that was an entirely different circumstance. They were back home now.

She couldn't bring herself to risk it.

"You must be hungry," she said instead. "I'd forgotten we missed dinner."

He turned slightly over his shoulder. "Actually, I was going to make sure to remove the pitcher of iced coffee Nonna keeps in here and drinks throughout the day. Based on what the doctor said, it's now off limits."

He was still worried. For all his strength and hardness, she'd never seen the vulnerability he'd shown while at the clinic.

"Then I want to go check on Enzo," he continued. "Unless you're concerned I may disturb him."

"No. But I've just left his room now. He's sleeping soundly."

"Good. Maybe I'll wait till morning then." He still hadn't shut the fridge door, still stood staring into its depths. She would bet he wasn't actually looking at anything.

"Are you sure you're not hungry? Can I prepare something for you? I can make a mean omelet."

"Your expert chef skills?"

She shrugged. "More that I just load it full of bacon and gooey, fatty cheese."

He let out a small laugh. "Maybe some other time."

Finally, he turned to face her. Against the backdrop of the light, shadows fell across his face. Even with such little light, she could see the tenseness of his features. He was barely holding on.

"Brianna?"

The timbre and longing in his voice sent a shiver down to her toes. "Yes?"

"You don't know how much it means that you were by my side tonight."

"Your grandmother is one of a kind, Marco. I was as scared as you were."

"Everything I know about love and acceptance I learned from that woman."

"I know."

"That is, until you and Enzo came along."

Brianna couldn't help her gasp. It was the closest Marco had ever come to admitting any kind of affection toward her. She had to wonder how much it had taken him to do so.

"Brianna?"

"Yes?"

"Would you please come here?"

Her feet seemed to move on their own. When she reached him, she knew she'd stopped breathing. Her pulse pounded in her veins. He lifted her chin gently with his finger and leaned in close. She didn't know what to expect, but it wasn't the soft, featherlight touch of his lips against hers. His kiss was gentle yet somehow full of passion at the same time.

Her hands moved up to his upper arms.

She knew what he was asking for. A respite from the world and all it had thrown on his shoulders when he was still too young and years before he was ready. He was asking for solace, for comfort.

She wanted that too, with him. With the only man she'd ever really cared for. He'd just admitted how much he cared for her too.

Warning bells rang in her head. After all, this was how it had all started, hadn't it? The first time they'd become intimate, Marco had turned to her for soothing and comfort. History was about to repeat itself, no denying it. Her heart might not be able to handle the fallout this time around. But she shoved those thoughts aside. Maybe she was being foolish, naive even. So be it. She loved him, she always had. She couldn't deny that fact any longer either.

Her husband needed her now. She wouldn't turn him down.

Her legs left the ground as he picked her up

and cradled her in his arms. All the while, he maintained the soul-shattering kisses she knew she might never recover from. Then he carried her upstairs.

"Good morning." Brianna opened her eyes to see Marco already showered and dressed. How did the man manage to summon so much energy? Particularly after the night they'd had? She herself could use a whole other night's sleep.

"You let me sleep late."

"I figured you needed it."

"But Enzo."

"Enzo is fine. I fed him his breakfast as soon as he awoke. And now he's playing quietly in his pen." He indicated the baby monitor across the room. Blessedly, all she could detect were the sounds of toddler play.

"See, there was no need to wake you. Enzo is fine. And Nonna is still resting comfortably. Plus, her appointment isn't for another few hours."

Brianna stretched and the silky sheet covering her slipped lower. She pulled it back up but not before Marco's eyes flickered over her bare skin. The heat in his eyes triggered a fluttering in her chest. Images from the night before assaulted her mind and her breath caught in her throat. "Then why are you dressed already?"

"That's a really good question. Now that I look at you, I feel I might have rushed a bit."

She resisted the urge to purr as he started to unbutton his shirt. There were times she hardly recognized herself around this man. This was one of those times.

She'd never been quite so brazen, so downright wanton with anyone else. But with Marco, that uncharacteristic streak had started the moment she'd laid eyes on him.

A nagging thought slithered into the back of her brain about all the questions that still plagued their relationship. All the times they'd fallen into each other's arms before only to turn around and have fate tamper or mar it in some way. She shook her head to eradicate the thought.

And she didn't even want to think about the regatta and what had happened there. The harsh truth was that none of the matters they'd been grappling with had altered in any way. Did that mean she had to focus on those issues entirely? Could she let herself, just for a while, focus instead on the current moment? Surely, the heavens wouldn't open up and the world wouldn't sink if she was just simply selfish for a bit.

Nonna had given them both quite a scare last night. Though her health scare seemed to be something that could be addressed, the episode had served to remind Brianna how temperamental life was. How fleeting any good fortune could be. It had also prompted Marco to finally confide in her in a way he never had before. So right now, she was only going to let herself focus on the here and now.

And right now, her husband had just crawled back into bed with her. It would serve her well to focus on that for as long as she could.

Before reality reared its head once more.

"That man is a quack. I don't think he even went to a decent medical school," Nonna declared as Marco assisted her into the back of the town car. He'd wanted to drive her to the appointment himself but she'd insisted being hauled around in that contraption he called a vehicle would trigger her heart palpitations again. As a result, he'd accompanied her in the back as Carlo drove them the twenty minutes to Dr. Gia's medical office.

She was not very happy with her long-term physician at the moment. Though the appointment had gone well, Nonna didn't like Dr. Gia's recommendations in the least. The one about the coffee and espresso elimination had been particularly ill met.

He would have to warn the household that Nonna's mood would border on unbearable as she adjusted. Marco sat down in the seat next to her and motioned for Carlo to start driving.

"He's been your physician for close to two decades, Nonna. You've never had a complaint before."

"Well, this is the first time he's lost his mind, that's why." Marco pinched the bridge of his nose. All that mattered was that it appeared she would be okay. With some medication and lifestyle changes, Nonna would be as good as new.

He didn't dare tell her that. Better to let her just vent. Not that he really blamed her. A lady her age would be set in her ways.

"Well, it appears the only pleasure or joy in my life will have to be provided by that great-grandson of mine," Nonna declared as Carlo shifted into gear. "Thank goodness for him at least."

At the mention of his son, an uneasiness settled into Marco's chest. Things between him and Brianna were confusing to say the least.

Her decision to move away again had been somewhat interrupted by Nonna's scare. But he didn't dare conclude that she'd changed her mind. The simple truth was he'd been too anxious to ask her, for fear that her answer would be that she still planned to leave.

He didn't want Nonna to have to find out the hard way if that was the case. He took a deep breath. "Enzo adores you too," he began. "And he's lucky to have you. But you know, you can have other interests and pursuits. Your garden for instance. And all your friends at church."

His grandmother turned in the seat to give him a steely glare. "Is there something you're trying to say, son?"

Perceptive as always, Marco thought, and tried to stifle a groan of frustration. This was really not the time or the place that he wanted to have this conversation. "I simply mean that there are other aspects of your life that can be sources of joy and comfort."

"Not like that little angel, there aren't. Now what are you getting at exactly?"

Better to just come out and say it. His grandmother wasn't one to let a matter drop when she had a strong opinion. Which was most of the time. "We can't assume that Enzo's permanent home will be here, Nonna."

"And why can't we? Are you trying to tell me you two are still having differences? That young lady didn't leave your side last night as you were waiting at the clinic."

"That doesn't necessarily mean anything."

"I believe it means a great deal."

"She was worried about you, Nonna. We can't read more into it than that."

"I believe she must have been concerned about you as well."

"Perhaps. We just have to be careful about making any assumptions."

She flung her hands up in the air in true Italian grandmother style. "I have a novel thought. You could just ask her. You know, tell her how you feel about her. See what she says in return. It's called having a conversation."

"Is one of the side effects of your new medications a penchant for sarcasm?"

"It's a serious question."

Marco sighed and looked out the window. "I'm not going to push her, Nonna. We both know there's no good to come of pursuing a woman who doesn't want to be pursued."

"Are we still on that, then?" She sounded disappointed, which in turn made him feel like the time when he'd been seven and had been caught stealing his cousin's gelato.

"Still on what?"

"Brianna is nothing like your mother. Not in the least."

Marco merely sighed. Any other time, he would have found a way to cut this conversation off. He was being indulgent because of what Nonna had gone through last night. But he had his limits, even under these circumstances.

"It happens to be the truth. And here's something else you haven't considered."

"What's that?"

"You are nothing like your father either. He

was my son, and I loved him with all my heart. But he expected to win at everything. And for most of his life, he did." Her voice shook as she continued. "Perhaps that was our fault. Perhaps we made life too easy for him at first. Being the only child, with your Nonno and me unable to have any more, he was the center of our universe. I admit we spoiled him. He was used to getting everything he wanted."

She huffed. "That was probably why he didn't know how to handle it the one time he didn't."

Marco considered her words for a moment. It was an angle he hadn't really considered. His papa's reaction had been just as important a factor as the way his mother had behaved.

"Have you heard of a *profezia auto-avverante*, son?" Nonna asked.

Of course he had. Loosely translated, it meant self-fulfilling prophecy.

CHAPTER FIFTEEN

"MISS BRIANNA, THERE'S a call for you. Overseas. From the States."

Brianna took the house phone Violetta handed her with mild curiosity. Who would have possibly tracked her here?

"Mrs. Dirici? This is Anton Seville, I'm Chef Ziyad's personal assistant." So she hadn't imagined that call back in New York before they'd left for Italy after all.

"Yes?"

"My deepest apologies. I know you were trying to get a hold of me a few weeks back and were unable to."

"This is quite a surprise, Mr. Seville."

"Please, call me Anton. Again, I'm sorry that we were unable to touch base. I was having some personal issues which made me somewhat inaccessible."

"How did you find me?"

"It took some sleuthing. Luckily, your surname is quite well known in the industry. But we searched New York first, your number was disconnected."

"I had to make an unexpected move," she explained, trying to control the excitement in her voice. One of the top chefs in New York had not only called her to begin with, but he'd instructed his assistant to search for her.

"So I've learned. I understand you're out of the country. Do you plan on returning to the States anytime soon? We'd like you to come into the restaurant."

Brianna cursed the air. Why was the timing in her life so often this misaligned? "I'm afraid I don't have any immediate plans at the time. Things are very...uncertain."

"I see. Perhaps you can send us some audition recipes then. And we can decide afterward where to go from there."

"I would love to."

Brianna's heart hammered. This was an opportunity she would be foolish to pass up. But it was truly a *Sliding Doors* moment. Her life had taken a drastic turn after Ziyad's initial phone call back in New York. She was here now, half a world away. With Marco and her son. Her circumstances had completely changed.

She'd been working her whole life for such a moment, but it was far from a cut-and-dried decision.

Still, what could it hurt to develop some audition recipes and send them over? At the very least, she'd learn if she had what it took to be hired by one of the best chefs on the East Coast.

With a myriad of conflicting emotions, she made her way to the kitchen and started pulling together ingredients, then took several pots out of the cabinets. An idea had taken hold already and a heady excitement took over as she started to work. Eventually, she was fully engrossed in the process.

She was still there three hours later when she heard the sound of the front door opening. Marco was home. His footsteps grew louder until he eventually appeared in the kitchen doorway.

"What is that delicious aroma? I swear I could smell it as soon as I turned past the gate into the property."

"Come, have a taste."

She dipped a spoon into the thick creamy sauce and reached it to his mouth.

"Mmm." True delight was clear in his voice and Brianna felt a pang of professional pride.

"That is really good, Brianna. Very creamy, though. Which one of Dirici's oils could you possibly incorporate into that?"

Brianna bit down on her cheek. He thought she was working on the marketing recipes they'd discussed several days ago.

"None, actually. This won't work with anything less than ghee."

He lifted an eyebrow in question. "Are you not working on a label addition then?"

Brianna's mouth had suddenly gone dry. The steam from the pots rose and swirled around them, adding a further ominousness to the air. "No, in fact this is for someone else."

"Someone?"

"I got a phone call today," she admitted. "From New York."

Understanding dawned in his eyes. Along with disappointment. Marco Dirici was a very smart man. "I think I can guess," he said and pushed his hair off his forehead with clear frustration.

"Chef Ziyad's assistant finally found me," Brianna blurted out, just to get it over with. "He wants me to send him some recipes."

"Because he'd still like to hire you."

"Yes."

A flurry of emotions flashed across Marco's face. Confusion, frustration, anger. Then she watched as he completely shut down. Again.

She had to try and clarify. "I'm just going to send him a couple of ideas. Simply to—"

"I leave you to it then." He turned to go but she rushed to catch him.

"Wait. I haven't made any kind of decision, Marco."

"Seems to me that you have." He tried to pull free but she gripped his arm tighter. He had to at least hear her out.

"No, that's not what this is."

"Is it not?" He pointed to the range and the saucepan that was now on the verge of boiling over. "Careful, you don't want to burn your sauce. That's going to look like Mount Etna any moment."

"Oh!" Brianna rushed to the stove and turned the dial to the off position. But she hadn't reached it in time. Sauce flooded over the side of the pan and poured onto the surface of the range like an erupting volcano. Gripping the handle with a holder, she managed to spill a few drops onto her wrist and gasped at the painful burn. "Ow!"

Great, her husband was livid. The kitchen looked like a scene out of a disaster movie. And the top of her hand was stinging with burns.

Yep, everything was a complete mess.

She brought her hand up and blew gently on the tender skin.

Marco stepped over to the counter beside her. "Is it bad, *cara*?"

"Nothing I haven't experienced before."

He took her hand gently and led her to the sink, held it under cold water where the hot liquid had splashed. Angry red welts had already formed above her knuckles.

"This is quite the mess, isn't it?" she said softly against his ear.

Marco looked up and their eyes locked. She could be referring to the kitchen or the whole sorry state of affairs.

"Quite."

But they had to tackle it. And they had no hope

of cleaning anything up if they didn't approach it together. Why couldn't he see that?

"Sometimes that's just what life hands you, Marco. Life itself is often messy and unruly with unexpected turns and sometimes events just spill over and someone gets burned."

She blew out a breath and leaned over to turn the tap off. Then added, "You can't control everything all the time."

"Is that what you think I try to do?"

"Most definitely."

He handed her a kitchen towel. "Well, it appears I'm failing miserably at it all then."

Marco leaned his forearms against the wooden rail of the veranda overlooking the gardens and the hills in the distance. Brianna was upstairs securing ointment to further protect her damaged skin. Thank heavens the burns were minor.

He'd been so excited when he'd walked in and the delicious aroma of her cooking had greeted him. He'd known right away that it was her doing rather than the cook's. Her style had a distinctive characteristic all its own. Just like her. Only to find out she was working to apply for a job back in the States.

Marco slammed his fist against the railing and bit out a curse. He'd known it. This was exactly what he'd been trying to explain to Nonna during the car ride.

Every time he harbored any kind of illusion that Brianna might be a steady fixture in his life, she threw him some kind of curve. Since he'd met her his life had been like a fairy tale shattered by harsh bursts of reality in between scenes.

It would drive him crazy. The same kind of madness that had driven his father to ruin all those years ago. Well, he wouldn't let it. His reaction would be very different. Unlike his father, he could be strong and determined. And he could move on.

He heard her tentative footsteps behind him and tried to control his temper.

"Marco?"

"Do you need another taste tester, *cara*? If so, I'm afraid you'll have to find someone else."

"That's not why I'm here."

"Then what is it?"

She came to stand next to him. For endless

seconds they both just stood side by side and stared at the scenery. At the beauty of Nonna's luscious, colorful flowers and bushes set against the backdrop of the dimming sunshine brought on by early evening.

"I simply wanted to send him some ideas, Marco. Just to see what he said. How could I have passed that up?"

"So you were merely looking for validation?"

He felt her shrug. "I suppose I was. Is that so wrong?"

"That's not something you want me to answer."

"That might be an answer in itself."

Marco pinched the bridge of his nose. Even now, he wanted to turn to face her. To take her in his arms and make her forget about that blasted phone call she'd received. A phone call that had sent their lives into yet another tailspin. "Then I have a question for you."

She let out a long, weary sigh. "What would that be?"

"What would you have done afterward? Once Ziyad gave you his answer?"

"Well, that would have depended on his answer."

Suddenly the frustration bubbling up within

his chest threatened to overflow. Like her saucepan. "Don't be coy with me, Brianna. You know what I'm asking. I think I have a right to ask it."

"Fair enough."

"You're not answering."

"I don't know, Marco. I don't want to deal with hypotheticals."

He almost wanted to laugh at that. "The man located you half a world away. Chances are he was going to ask you to come work for him. The recipe was probably just a formality."

"Maybe you're right." She hesitated and he knew what she was going to say next, though he desperately hoped to be wrong. "I guess I would have wanted to see about accepting."

Marco felt something in his heart give way. He wasn't surprised. But the disappointment cut sharper than it should have. He should have known better than to let her get under his skin again. A family was just not in the cards for him. Not as a child. And not as an adult.

"But I wouldn't have just made the decision and then hoisted my choices onto your shoulders," she implored.

"What exactly does that mean?"

"It means we could have talked it over. Together. We could have discussed the pros and cons. Tried to come to some sort of mutual understanding."

"We would have fought."

She blew out a puff of frustration, turned to him. "This is what I mean about hypotheticals. All of this is moot until and if I actually get any kind of offer."

Did she even realize she was practicing clear avoidance?

He'd had enough. They could keep going around like this in circles. With Brianna there would always be the next potential opportunity, the next pursuit.

The next chance to escape. Just like his mother.

His temper spiked further. "You want to tell me that we can discuss things as a couple, come to a mutual decision. Is that right?"

"That's exactly what I'm saying."

"Then why didn't you tell me you were going to send in your recipes? Why was *that* not a matter of discussion?"

She actually stomped her foot. "You weren't

even home! I had an idea and I just wanted to get started."

"Right." He stood upright and pivoted on his heel. Another useless conversation that was getting them nowhere. Marco felt tired. And angry. He hadn't even had a chance to change out of his work clothes. Whether she wanted to admit it or not—even to herself—Brianna had already made all sorts of decisions without consulting her husband.

"Don't walk away, Marco. It's what you always do."

She didn't understand. He had to walk away or things between them would take one of two turns. They'd either say things there would be no coming back from. Or they would fall into each other's arms. Neither scenario produced any kind of a lasting happy ending.

"It's been a long day, *cara*. And I believe you should tend to that burn some more."

"That can wait. It's not so bad anymore. I just want you to understand."

"Understand what exactly?"

"What it would mean to someone like me to be able to say I made it as a master chef one day.

In one of the most competitive markets of the world, no less."

"Oh, but I do understand. You've told me countless times."

Her cheeks grew red with anger. "If you really did understand, you wouldn't have just said that. Why can't we ever just have a civil conversation? Just to hammer some things out?"

Why was she doing this? Why was she taunting him? Didn't she realize how close he was to the edge?

"You are not the kind of woman who wants her man to be civil, *cara*." He had no logical reason to say such a thing. He'd done it just to throw her off balance. He ignored the shame that came with admitting that to himself. But not the satisfaction that the comment seemed to hit the mark.

That seemed to take her back a step. "Stop that."

"Stop what?"

"Stop turning what I say into something seductive. I'm trying to have a conversation with you here."

"Is that what you're trying to do?"

"Yes. I'm trying to see if we can maturely, like

adults, come to a solution about what was obviously a too hasty decision."

"Right. Your moving here. You appear to regret it now."

Her lower lip dropped. "Me? *I* appear to regret it? You've been a miserable troll just because you saw me working on some recipes. Don't even pretend differently."

He didn't know whether he was supposed to deny that. Was she looking for reassurance? If anything, that was too weak a word. He was beyond miserable. And he was beyond angry. More so at himself than anyone else. "So let's just decide what we want and work to rectify things."

What he wanted was to somehow go back to that day at the pond. When she'd been laughing and joking with him as they both played with their son. He wanted to somehow hold that moment in time and suspend it forever.

Marco bit his lip. This was ridiculous. He had to get away from her now. "Fine. Then work it out."

"What? Work what out?"

"You heard me. Ask the experts when it's safe for you and Enzo to return to the States."

"What?"

"That's what you want."

"I didn't say that's what I wanted."

"Because you don't really know. You never did. But I'm tired of arguing. Just figure out how quickly you're able to get back to New York." He bit out a curse. "You're right. Having two confused and warring parents is not in Enzo's best interest. We might be doing him a favor in the long term."

She raised her hands, palms up. "So that's it. I should just see about leaving with Enzo?"

Marco nodded, not even certain of what he was saying any more. He just wanted to get out of this conversation, get out of this house.

"Find your child psychologist. I'll put all the resources Dirici Foods has to ensure he gets the best professional money can buy. And I'll make sure he knows his papa will be a constant presence in his life. Just do what you have to do, Brianna. And then leave me alone."

She was shocked enough to let him pass this time. Marco raced upstairs for his car keys. He didn't want to think about what he'd just said. Or what he would do if Brianna took him at his word. Right now, he just wanted some fresh air.

A long drive along the curvy stone cliff roads leading to town. Then perhaps he could drown his confusion in one of the bars there. It seemed like a good night to spend in a hotel.

He reached his suite and threw open the closet door to change into some fresher clothes. Something tugged at his attention and he glanced at the dresser drawer beneath the television. It always tugged at his attention but he never actually took it out. He should get rid of it, tear it up. Had meant to years ago. All the others had been disposed of.

Today. Right now. He pulled open the bottom drawer and pulled out the piece of paper, wilting and discolored due to constant handling by a small child years ago.

There was no need to hold on to it. No sentimental reasons, none due to happy memories.

He tore it into more than a dozen pieces. A mysterious letter he'd received from his mother about eighteen months after she'd left, telling him about her travels and her plans to visit again. A visit that never happened. The previous one had been the final time he'd seen her.

Then had come word decades later that she had passed.

It was about time he destroyed the letter. The last remaining reminder of Antonia Dirici. He should have destroyed it years ago, along with her photos.

Brianna chose that moment to step quietly into the room. "What was that?"

Marco bristled at the question. But he would answer it. "A letter. From *mi madre*. Right after she left for the last time."

He pointed to the shredded pieces of paper on the floor. "That's what broke my father finally and for good. Her sending me that letter left no doubt that she wouldn't be coming back. Not that time."

"Yet you kept it all these years."

"To remind myself. Of exactly what she did to him. So that I would never forget."

Brianna's words when she spoke were soft but firm.

"I didn't know him at all, but I have no doubt whatsoever that you're a much stronger man than your father."

"Then why did you leave?" He wasn't sure

which one of them was more shocked at the question. He had no idea he'd intended to ask it. Let alone that he'd been thinking it.

He turned to study her. Brianna did indeed look as if at a loss for words. Finally, she found her voice. "We had a lot working against us, Marco. We were both unprepared."

"I wouldn't argue with any of that."

"Nor can you deny that you were not in a good place when you first met me. You were dealing with the news of your mother having just died."

He simply nodded.

"One of the many things you never told me, that you never shared."

"There was no point."

She sucked in a deep breath. "The point was that I was your wife. But you weren't really looking for one. You were looking simply for solace. Maybe even just a distraction."

"And what of you, *cara*? If I recall, you were nursing some wounds yourself. Your relationship had just abruptly ended. Would you have found yourself in my arms otherwise?"

"Maybe not. We clearly didn't give any of it

enough thought. But the difference was, I was willing to try."

He quirked an eyebrow at her. "And you don't think I was?"

Her eyes started to glisten with tears and he wanted to kick himself. But all of this needed to be said. Here and now. Though her next words seemed to be causing her physical pain as she said them. "You clearly weren't ready to share your life with someone, Marco. Certainly not someone like me."

CHAPTER SIXTEEN

BRIANNA HEARD MARCO'S sports car roar to life and drive away from the garage toward the main gate. He hadn't told her where he was going, or how long he'd be gone. Nonna was resting. The staff were all busy. And Enzo was winding down before dinner.

She felt utterly alone. Unable to bear the solitude after her argument with Marco, she made her way to the door to head for the vineyards. She had to get out of this house the same way Marco had.

She didn't know how much time had passed when she heard a cheery masculine voice behind her. "We have got to stop meeting like this."

"Leo!" She turned and gave him a tight hug. Leo was one of those few people who could lighten the darkest mood. That was exactly what she needed right now.

"What are you doing here?" she asked him.

"I brought over some papers for Marco to sign. But it turns out he's not home."

"No, and I don't know when he'll be back."

Leo's smile faltered almost imperceptibly but he didn't ask any questions. "Then as I was driving past the vines, I saw you strolling along. Thought I'd stop by and say hello."

"I'm so glad you did."

"Need me to drive you back home again?"

She was nowhere near ready to return to the house, still needed the fresh air. "Actually, I'd like it much more if you walked with me a bit."

Leo held out his arm for her to take. "It would be an honor."

Slipping her hand into the crook of his elbow, she took the lead and resumed walking. "I never got a chance to apologize to you," she told him.

He squinted at her. "Whatever do you need to apologize for?"

"That day at the harbor. Before the regatta. I was horribly ill. I know it dampened the mood and probably ruined everyone's time." It had certainly ruined Marco's.

"Of course you don't have to apologize for that, dear. You can't help getting sick."

She wanted to kiss him on the cheek for his kindness. He'd never been anything less since she'd met him. Why couldn't she have fallen for someone like Leo? He was sweet-natured, light-hearted, with a good sense of humor. So unlike her husband.

And so not in any way enticing to her. Again, also very unlike her husband. She had to face it, she'd been drawn to that man without any hope of being able to resist.

"Still, it wasn't how I wanted to meet Marco's sailing friends for the first time."

"Those are more than just sailing friends. We've all known each other since childhood. They will most certainly understand."

"That Marco is married to someone who clearly doesn't belong?"

Leo stopped in his tracks, forcing her to halt midstride as well. "Brianna? Is there something specific on your mind?"

Brianna felt the sting of tears and bit the inside of her cheek from crying on Leo's shoulder right then and there.

"Isn't it obvious? I was like a complete fish out of water that day. If you'll pardon the pun."

Leo gave her a gentle smile.

"You just have to get used to the sea. It takes some people longer than others. We all grew up on it, including Marco. Sometimes we forget others are more landlocked."

"You're a kind soul, Leo. But none of that erases that fact that Marco has much more in common with people such as yourself and—" She made herself stop. This was so useless.

"And?"

She should stop this right now. At the least she was going to sound like a jealous insecure besotted fool, something she'd swore she would never be.

"And say for instance the ladies who were there that day. Like Talia for example."

Suddenly, understanding dawned on Leo's face. "Ah, I see," he said and looked away. Then he shocked her by laughing out loud.

"Shouldn't you be having this conversation with your husband?" he asked mid-laugh.

Ouch. He was right. She'd been too cowardly to do so. "You're right. Of course."

Leo's expression suddenly turned serious. More serious than she'd ever seen him. "I hope I'm not overreaching here, *mi tesoro*. But I've known

Marco since we were both babes and…let's just say he can be complicated."

That was certainly putting it mildly. Brianna had to try hard not to roll her eyes. "Oh, I've definitely discovered that little fact on my own."

"He's also one of the most loyal men I've ever met. It's a rare quality these days."

Brianna inhaled deeply, taking in the sweet scent of the flowers and vines. "I just want to understand him, Leo. He doesn't make it easy."

Leo rubbed his chin. "No, I'm sure he doesn't. But maybe it will be enough to understand this—he's never been as happy as he has since little Enzo arrived. He truly loves that boy and relishes his role as a father."

He wasn't telling her anything she didn't know. Marco had done everything he could to make sure their son knew he was a cherished and loved child. She couldn't have hoped for more in that regard.

Leo went on before she could respond. "I've also never seen him so taken by a woman."

That statement did in fact surprise her. Leo was simply just trying to charm her, as was his nature. "Come on, Leo. I'm sure a man like Marco has had multiple liaisons. I'm not naïve."

Leo gave her a mischievous wink. "I didn't say he was a saint. But he's never acted so…affected, let's say."

She affected Marco?

Leo rubbed a gentle hand on her shoulder, the way an older sibling might to reassure a younger one. "Don't sell yourself short as far as your husband is concerned, love. I know my friend well and have no doubt that he cares deeply for you. You shouldn't either."

The sun had yet to set when Marco returned home. The drive had done him worlds of good. But unsettled feelings still churned in his gut. He made a beeline to his son's suite. He hadn't seen the boy all day and was dearly missing him. It was one thing to have him far away when he was a baby, but now that the boy was older he was such a sight to observe. Marco would be doing a lot of business in his New York offices if Brianna ended up back there.

At this point, that seemed very likely. Eventually, Brianna was going to make her way back to America. All signs pointed in that direction. Unless he did something about it. Unless he told her that it was the last thing he wanted.

He found Enzo in the tub. Brianna sat next to him as he played with an armada of plastic boats. He was up to his little armpits in foamy bubbles.

Brianna gave him a tentative smile when he walked in. Too weary to engage with her yet again, he simply motioned to his son. "Do you mind if I take over?"

Brianna stood. "Uh. Sure. He just got in though. He'll be a while, the ships have a lot of maneuvers to complete."

"That's fine. I'd like some time with him." Maybe the soothing presence of his son would help him pull some of his thoughts together, give him some kind of action plan.

She appeared on the verge of saying something else. Then seemed to think better of it.

"Certainly." Handing him a baby towel, she walked out the bathroom door.

Marco crouched down on his knees by the side of the tub. Enzo gave his father a wide smile then shoved a boat under the water.

"That's not a submarine, little man." The innocuous comment earned him a loud giggle.

"This one is," he said and plucked one of the toys out of the water.

"Toot. Toot."

It was Marco's turn to laugh. "Submarines don't—" He stopped himself from making the correction. To a boy Enzo's age, submarines could absolutely make train noises. The world was endless, the possibilities limitless. He would try to instill that belief system in his son.

He picked up another boat and held it in front of Enzo. "What sound does this one make?"

The boy actually roared.

Marco gave his hair a tousle. "There's something I want you to know," he told him even though he knew Enzo was too young to understand what he was about to say. "I want you to know Papa loves you. And he always will."

"Papa!" Enzo repeated with gusto.

"That's right. No matter how big you get, I'll always be your papa. Do you understand?"

Enzo nodded so enthusiastically his chin hit the water.

"Good. Remember that always."

Enzo would never be lacking a father. Marco had learned firsthand how important that was.

A soft knock at the door pulled him out of his thoughts. "I thought you might need some help getting him out and dry," Brianna said, sticking her head through the door.

"That'd be great, thanks."

As she stepped in with the towel, Marco lifted the boy up and placed him in his mother's arms. For one brief moment, their eyes locked. Marco had a strange urge to tell her all the things he'd just spoken to his son. Brianna needed to hear them too.

He should have said them long ago, when little Enzo was first born. He wanted her to understand that there were some things he was just barely coming to terms with himself. In his efforts to avoid falling into the trap his father had, Marco had subconsciously chosen avoidance. Rather than confront his fears of being a bad father himself, he had chosen to stay away. He'd learned as a child that it was easier and better for everyone involved if you kept your emotions in check.

Except that approach hadn't exactly worked out for him where Brianna was concerned. So he had to make the effort. He had to find a way to tell her that he would try. He would do everything he could to not only become a better husband and father but also a better man. And he would do it for her.

Brianna clutched Enzo to her chest and turned away as she nuzzled his cheek.

And the words escaped him. Yet another moment to say anything was gone.

CHAPTER SEVENTEEN

SHE'D NEVER BEEN this nervous preparing a meal before. Brianna glanced at the kitchen clock hanging on the wall above the sink. Marco would be home soon and it looked like she had pretty much timed everything perfectly.

The birds were ready to come out of the oven, the wine had been suitably aired, the salad adequately chilled. She had just enough time to shower and dress while the main course cooled. Thank the heavens.

He would be pleased. He had to be.

Though if she were being honest with herself, she had to admit this was as much for her as it was for her husband. Meal preparation had become almost a chore for her, part of her career aspirations. She had let her professional ambitions color the entire reason she'd wanted to become a chef in the first place. For the sense of home and family inherent in sharing a meal with loved ones.

Sighing, she took off the stained apron and undid her hair as she made her way up the stairs.

Yes, this evening was about more than simply preparing a meal. Hopefully, Marco would see that too. This was about Brianna Stedman proving her skills, her determination, and the sheer number of obstacles she'd overcome in her life.

So while Marco might not share much in common with her in terms of background or privilege, maybe that wasn't so bad. Maybe that was what had drawn them together in the first place.

Maybe it was what would keep them together.

Brianna was waiting for him when Marco walked through the door after returning from the office. Whatever she had in mind, Marco wasn't sure he was up for it.

It had been a hell of a day. A simple deal had hit all sorts of snags and one of his vendors had threatened not to renew a very lucrative contract. The type of contract that would immediately affect his profit margin if Dirici Foods lost it. He couldn't allow that to happen. Marco would now have to fly out to Paris as soon as he could to meet with the man personally. So he wasn't quite ready with a response when his estranged wife greeted him as he entered.

But then he noticed she was dressed up. Very dressed up. In a sleek, shimmery little black dress that fit her form like a glove. A pink pearl choker adorned her neck. Her hair was piled atop her head with just enough wisps escaping to soften the effect.

She took his breath away. Marco had to tighten his hands into fists to keep from reaching for her. A better man would have figured out how to keep a lady like her by his side. A better man would have moved heaven and earth to make the marriage to her work out. He'd failed.

"Are you going somewhere?" he asked her.

Her smile was subtle, her lips curved in a sensual way. "Yes, as a matter of fact. But it's not far."

He'd never be able to figure this woman out. "And do you need something from me before you go?"

She walked over and took him by the arm. "You're coming with me."

What was she playing at? He really was in no mood for any shenanigans after the day he'd had.

If she knew him even a little, she would have sensed that.

"Brianna, I've had a rather long day. I just want to eat some dinner—"

She cut him off by actually touching a finger to his lips. The unexpected contact sent a shock wave through his cells. She hadn't so much as touched him in days.

"That's exactly what we're going to do," she told him. But instead of the main dining room, she led him over to the veranda.

What greeted him there looked like something out of a foodie magazine spread. A table covered in white linen sat where normally the patio lounge furniture would be. A warm, comfortable fire had been started in the fire pit. The table had been set with full place settings.

For two.

Brianna reached for a bottle of Cabernet sitting on a side table and began pouring it.

Well, this was all unexpected. "What is this?"

"Dinner."

Okay... "Where is everyone?"

"Nonna took Enzo with her to visit some of

the ladies from church. And I gave everyone the day off."

Marco couldn't guess what she was up to. Nor could he quite figure out what to make of it. Deciding the easiest course would be to just let her explain, he shrugged off his jacket and tossed it on one of the chairs.

"I know it's a little earlier than our regular dining time, but I don't know how long Nonna and Enzo will be gone." She handed him a full glass of wine then held hers up. "Cheers."

The explanation wasn't forthcoming any time soon, it appeared. Marco took a large swig of his drink.

Setting his glass down he met her eyes. "Brianna, what is this?" he repeated.

"I told you. We are having dinner." She motioned for him to sit. He did so and she took the seat across from him. Several covered platters and bowls sat in the center of the table.

She cleared her throat. "It occurred to me that the only meals I've ever made for you were entrees like lasagna or *piccatta*. Or something along those lines."

"And?"

"My specialty is Spanish tapas. With some Mediterranean fusion incorporated, I've trained extensively to perfect such meals. Or I was before we…met."

Marco steepled his hands in front of his face as she started serving. "Is this some kind of attempt to convince me of your talent? Because I assure you it's hardly necessary. I don't even see the point—"

She cut him off. "This is arugula and basil salad with candied pecans and aged feta cheese. It's our first course. This won't be the traditional Italian menu. Like I said, as luck would have it, that's not my specialty."

"Am I to just accept that you woke up this morning and decided that what you wanted to do most today was cook for the two of us?"

"I've actually been thinking about it since we argued."

She had? "You're serious. You just up and decided that the thing we needed right now was to have you prepare a meal so that we could eat together?"

She nodded, swallowed her bite of salad and took another sip of her wine. "Partly. Our main course is to be young game hen with a raspberry coulis sauce and a side of truffle creamed paella. As for dessert, that's also not in my area of expertise. Therefore I just ran out for some chocolate gelato earlier this afternoon."

Yet another evasion. Was she trying to make him crazy? Here she was talking about gelato and game hens when he had no idea what was happening between them at the moment. "What do you mean 'partly'?"

She slowly set her fork down on the side of her plate. "We never really had romantic dinners, or date nights, or even went to the movies for that matter. Did we, Marco?"

"No, I guess we didn't." He was starting to see her point. What little he and Brianna knew about one another, even after all this time, had been learned on the fly. After they were already husband and wife. Almost like a modern-day arranged marriage.

A spark ignited in his chest. She was making an effort. It surprised him how touched he was.

"Do you want to know why I became a chef, Marco."

He swallowed. "Very much so."

"Remember that foster mother I was telling you about?"

"The ex-dancer?"

She smiled at him, clearly pleased that he remembered. "Yes, that's the one. See, she had this routine. Despite all her faults, she was good to me and the other children. Her lifestyle wasn't the best but she did a lot of things right."

"Such as?"

"Such as always making sure we had a warm meal. Every evening, no matter what was happening, she ensured something hot was on the table."

"She sounds like a remarkable woman."

"She was. I lost touch with her over the years. After a while, it was too painful to keep in contact." She gave a small shrug of her shoulders. "And she didn't try very hard either. Who knows, maybe my days in her home meant more to me than they did to her." Her eyes glistened with tears. "The day they pulled me out of that house, the most secure, stable one I'd ever been in, I swore I would never forget the importance of having that meal on the table."

"I'm glad you've finally told me."

"I should have told you before." She wiped away the moisture from her eyes with the back of her hand. "I realize now that I put too much in your hands. You weren't exactly ready for marriage and a child either." She chewed the inside of her cheek. "It's just that you've always seemed so strong to me, so capable. I figured I'd lay most of the burden on your shoulders. But now I've come to realize that I'm both those things as well."

She picked up her fork again, but didn't continue eating. Just sort of twirled it around her fingers. When she spoke again her voice was stronger, more firm. "You were right that I wasn't very open myself. See, I thought I had an excuse. I was ashamed. Embarrassed about who I was and how I'd grown up. But that doesn't matter. I'm me. I may not know much about Italian cooking. I'd like to work on that."

"Bree, you don't need to—"

She cut him off with a wave of her hand. "I want to. But in the meantime, I'd like you to discover and enjoy what I do have to offer."

Marco's mouth went dry. His wife was one brave and remarkable woman. How could he have ever doubted that about her? How could he have doubted her strength or resilience?

He owed it to her to be brave in return.

The parallels in their respective pasts were striking if one thought about it. Why she was so determined to make her own way, to be successful in her own right. Also the reason she was so afraid that their marriage might not be successful long-term.

Whatever it took, he would prove to her that it could.

She took a large gulp of her wine and looked into his eyes. "So you see, Marco. We're much more alike than you would have ever guessed. It appears we both need to draw on some patience until we figure all this out. Are you willing to do that? With me?"

His mind went numb, he had to scramble for the right words. "Yes, *cara*. More than anything. And there's no one else I'd rather share my life or a child with."

A wealth of emotion cascaded over her face. "We're so lucky to have our boy, aren't we? And he's growing up so fast."

He couldn't help his grin of pride. "Like an active vine during harvest. Bree, I don't want either of us to miss a moment of it. I want both of us to be there for him when he attends his first day of nursery school, when he makes his first best friend." He gave a mock shudder. "When he throws his first pitch of a baseball."

"I want all that too," she said with a rasp. "It's all I've ever wanted. To truly live as a family. With our son."

Marco itched to go to her, to lift her in his arms. He forced himself to remain seated instead. There was so much more he owed it to her to say. "But Enzo deserves a mother who feels fulfilled."

Her eyes grew wide. "What are you saying?"

"I don't want you to give up your dreams, Bree." He took a deep breath, steadying himself to say his next words. "If you still want to make a name for yourself in New York, we'll find a way. We'll make it happen."

Her eyes filled with tears once more. "You don't know how much that means to me, Marco. But I've been thinking. And I've had a change of heart."

He could only blink at her. After all her training, all her drive, she couldn't mean she was ready to give up her career. "You have?"

She nodded. "Working on those marketing recipes gave me a taste of what it would be like to be independently employed."

"I don't understand."

"I'd like to keep coming up with recipes for your product line. If you could still use them."

She had no idea. "Of course. But will that be enough for you, Bree? That was meant to be just a temporary plan."

"I've also got some ideas for another project."

"What kind of project?"

Her face lit up like a child on Christmas morning as she began to speak. "I'd like to work on a cookbook. To be published under my maiden name." She searched his face. "So there isn't any influence based on the Dirici brand. You do understand that, don't you?"

Rather than answer, he stood and walked around the table. Gently taking her hand, he pulled her up to stand next to him.

"*Si*. And there's something I'd like you to understand."

"What's that?" she asked as he took her by the waist and pulled her to him.

"That about three years ago, when I inadvertently walked into that kitchen, I met the woman I was supposed to spend the rest of my life with. The woman I was meant to fall in love with."

Brianna sucked in a breath and leaned against him. "And I met the man of my dreams. The man I've been in love with ever since."

As if on cue, the fire behind them sparked, sending bright golden embers shooting into the air. He watched over Brianna's head as they drifted and fluttered on the breeze.

"There's one more thing," he added, rubbing her cheek. "I just decided I really rather like poultry served cold." Then he took her lips with his own.

"You do, huh?" she whispered, breathless from his kiss.

"*Si*. And another thing, I don't want dessert either." He took her by the hand and headed inside. "Not until much, much later," he added, as he led her upstairs.

EPILOGUE

HOW IN THE world had she been talked into this? Brianna took Marco's hand and allowed him to help her up the steps and onto the boat. Immediately, she felt a small tickle at the bottom of her stomach. They hadn't even left the slip yet.

"I don't know about this," she declared and gripped his fingers tighter.

"It will be all right, *cara*. Trust me."

"If you say so."

He pulled her up against him, his back to her chest. Then he tilted her chin up to look out at the ocean. "There are lots of ways to avoid the seasickness. I'll show you."

Brianna bit back the apprehension that only served to make her nausea worse. "Fine. What do you suggest?"

"Okay, first of all, keep looking at the distance. It's like being up high. Do not look down."

"All right. What else."

"Keep your knees slightly bent."

He couldn't be serious with this, could he? "My knees?"

He nodded against her cheek. "*Si, cara.* It helps to maintain your center of balance."

She did as she was told. "What else?"

"As soon as you feel an inkling of dizziness, pinch the inside of your palm." He took her hand and demonstrated. "Do that as often as necessary. All that will certainly help."

"That's it?" she asked, incredulous. "That's all I need to know to keep the seasickness under control?"

He seemed to think for a moment. "Wait. There is one more thing." He reached into his pocket and pulled out a small plastic bottle. The label had Italian lettering and pictures of a plane and a ship. "You should also just take one of these. Then you won't have to do all that other stuff I just told you. It's all actually pretty useless."

Motion sickness medicine.

Brianna gave him a playful slap on the hand. "Ha-ha. Very funny."

He kissed her then, and she felt the heat clear through her core. The man's effect on her would

be her undoing. And she would love every minute of it.

"I'm serious," Marco told her. "You need to
have a good supply of these on hand. A good
portion of our honeymoon will involve quite a
bit of sailing."

Had she heard him correctly? This morning,
he'd surprised her with an invitation to the marina,
so she could get accustomed slowly to being on
the water. Was it possible this was more than that?

"Honeymoon?"

"It occurs to me we never really took an official one. I'd like to rectify that."

Words failed her. The act was so thoughtful,
so heartfelt she felt tears spring to her eyes. She
didn't realize Marco had actually cared about
the informal and rather rushed way they'd begun
their marriage. "I'd like that very much."

"There's also something else I'd like to rectify."

"What's that?"

"I never actually offered you a proper proposal," he said, then shocked her by getting down
on one knee.

Reaching once more into his pocket, he pulled
out a small velvet box. Then opened it to reveal

a shimmering emerald surrounded by diamonds on a delicate gold chain.

Enzo's birthstone.

Marco cleared his throat, his voice hoarse when he spoke. "You already have a ring. So I thought this might be more appropriate."

Brianna's fingers trembled as she reached for it. "Oh, Marco. It's lovely." So beyond merely appropriate, this delicate piece of jewelry was the perfect symbol of the renewed bond of their marriage as well as their devotion to their child. He had put so much thought into the gesture.

"Brianna Dirici, would you please do me the honor of marrying me? Again?"

"Yes!" She kissed him with all the love and all the elation that was currently bursting through her heart. "I would be honored to marry you! Again and again and—"

She didn't get a chance to say any more.

* * * * *

LET'S TALK
Romance

For exclusive extracts, competitions
and special offers, find us online:

 facebook.com/millsandboon

 @millsandboonuk

 @millsandboon

Or get in touch on 0844 844 1351*

For all the latest titles coming soon,
visit millsandboon.co.uk/nextmonth

*Calls cost 7p per minute plus your phone company's price per
minute access charge